INKED

A KILL DEVIL INK NOVEL

SARAH DARLINGTON

INKED

Copyright © 2020 Sarah Darlington

Cover Design TE Black Designs

Editing by Kamaryn Kretz

To all the KILL DEVIL HILLS and NEVER TRUST fans out there! I wrote this one for you. Thank you for your continued support.

~ CHAPTER 1 ~

NICK

"Is this an impulse decision?" the girl with pink hair and a tattoo gun in her hand asked me. "You sure you're sober? I can't do this if you aren't sober."

I turned to look over my shoulder. My bare ass was on display for the room, for this pink haired beauty to glimpse, and neither was a concern. I felt like I was stuck, buried deep under the sand. I'd felt that way for a couple weeks now, maybe longer if I were being honest with myself. I hoped this small amount of pain might shock my senses somehow, help me feel something again. At the very least, this was a parting gift... *to me from myself.* Tonight was my final night in town. Tomorrow I planned to quit my job and drive back to Maine.

Good riddance, Kill Devil Hills.

"Not an impulse decision," I clarified. "I'm sober."

"It's just... it's a sea turtle on your ass." She gave me this pained look. "On your virgin skin, no less. I feel like I should make sure this is really, *really*, what you want."

"What do most guys get? Barbed wire around their biceps. No thank you, sweetheart. I know what I want. This is what I want."

She bit down on her bottom lip, giving me a reluctant nod. Shit, she was a beautiful girl. I loved her pale pink hair color. For a brief second, I wondered what her story was. Was she from this beach town, born and raised, or had she escaped here just like I had, thinking it was the solution to everything, when it really wasn't?

I rested my face on my forearms, lying still for her, waiting for her to get started. Finally, the needle hit my skin. It stung. But it was a very bearable kind of pain.

I don't know if it helped or hurt the dull ache in my chest. After a couple minutes, my butt cheek just felt numb. I felt numb along with it.

"So why the turtle?" the girl asked.

I sighed. "C'mon, this isn't a hair salon." Again, I glanced over my shoulder. "You don't have to bother with small talk. Not with me."

She looked at me with these big, kind of sad, brown eyes. I'd offended her. Fuck. I hadn't meant to do that.

"Hey." One of the other tattoo artists that worked at this place stepped into her area. "I'm going to pop next door and get some dinner. Want something, Amanda?"

"No," she muttered. "Not hungry."

He turned his attention to me. "You're probably going to be on that table for a couple hours. Want some dinner? The place next door is actually decent."

I cleared my throat. "No, thanks."

"Alrighty." The massive guy with tattoos up to his neck stepped away. It wasn't a busy night. Without him here, it would be just the two of us.

I dropped my head back to my arms. I heard the bell on the door chime as he exited the shop. "He's stupid," I mumbled into my arms. Her name was Amanda. Thanks to Meat Head, I now knew my pink haired tattoo artist's name was Amanda. "It's stupid for him to leave you by yourself. It's just us. It's late. Even if it's only for ten minutes, something could happen in those ten minutes. You don't know how many creeps there are in this world. In the future, you should make him get the place next door to walk your food over."

My words were probably out of bounds. I'd never been great at minding my own business. But it *was* stupid. To leave her alone with one of her customers this late in the evening—plain dumb.

"I hate this sea turtle," she suddenly said. She stopped working, setting down the tattoo gun, peeling off her gloves. "I hate it. Like in the past year I've probably done this same sea turtle six other times. Exact copies. All of them on eighteen-year-old girls who don't have a clue what they want. The kind of girls who walk into the store not knowing what they want and just pick out the first pretty thing they see on the wall. Fuck, it's lame. Come with me."

"What?"

"Pull up your pants. Come with me."

I had no choice. She had already left me behind. I glanced down at the ink on my skin. She'd barely even begun. I jumped off the table, yanking up my jeans over the tiny black blob on my ass, and I followed her. She led me deeper into the shop, past a couple other unoccupied stations, toward a back room. It looked more like a break room than anything. She sat at a computer, patting the chair next to her.

Hesitantly, I sat down beside her. *Had she gained nothing from my lecture on safety and strangers?* I guess not.

After a moment waiting on the computer to boot itself up, she typed "sea turtle tattoos" into Google, and started scrolling through images. "The designs from the wall, the ones that John has drawn," she started talking. I didn't know who John was, I guessed maybe the owner of this place? Her boss? "They're great designs, beautiful designs, but none of them very unique." This coming from a woman with mostly flowers on her skin. Bubbly, colorful flowers. "Because anyone who walks in the front door can look at John's art and choose that turtle off the wall. You'll be on the beach this summer, and I promise you'll see someone walk by with your same turtle on her shoulder. Or on her foot. Maybe on her ass, just like you."

I'd be in Maine this summer. But even if I were here, it would be the least of my concerns. "Maybe I'll find my soulmate that way," I muttered. "We can have matching turtle ass tattoos and ride off into the sunset together."

She smiled at my dry humor. Which was amazing in itself because most people never got my jokes, when I made those 'true to myself' kind of jokes. "I have an idea." She left me and the computer. At the table in the room, she grabbed a piece of plain white paper. She began to sketch something. Her own turtle. It wasn't at all what I had in mind when I decided I wanted this tattoo. The one I'd chosen from John's wall of art was truer to real life. But her version—it was made up of all these cuts and lines. Completely abstract. It was a piece of art. I don't know why, but I instantly loved it. Something about it spoke to me. And then the shell of the turtle, instead of giving it a normal shell, she gave it sails. It was half turtle and half pirate ship. Who knows what the fuck it was? But I loved it. I loved it fiercely. I wanted this on my skin.

She shrugged when she finished, passing over her design to me.

I took the paper. "I like it. Let's do this."

"It's weird. I know."

"It is weird, but I'm choosing this. Can you put it on my ass now, Amanda? Please?"

Again, she smiled at me. Damn, she had a pretty smile. "One turtle ass tattoo coming right up."

~ CHAPTER 2 ~

AMANDA

This guy was strange. Like *'super, impossible-to-figure-out, this-conundrum-will-drive-me-insane'* kind of strange.

So far, I'd gathered that he was wealthy. Like, super wealthy. Like, if he told me he was some famous actor, I wouldn't have been surprised. I could smell it on him. Like, literally, as I pressed the tattoo gun to his fair skin, I thought this in my head. I'd never smelled anyone who smelled as good as this guy. It had to be what money fucking smelled like. I wouldn't know, I'd never had much in that department, but he smelled like he cost a fortune.

Then his sea turtle choice. I mean... what? Why? Seriously, of all things, why would a guy want that? He had no other ink on his skin. He had virgin skin. So why one lonely sea turtle as his first tattoo? Why on this random Wednesday night had he walked into this tattoo shop wanting that of all things?

I'd also hijacked his tattoo. I'd called it lame after he gave me that small, annoying lecture on my safety. Then I'd drawn something I never thought he'd be into. Sometimes my brain worked in pictures. I'd see images in real life, and I'd want to chop them up, rearrange them, make them into something new. Most days, here at work, I stuck to the book, copied John's artwork onto people's skin, and never deviated. But tonight I'd deviated. And it floored me that this white-collar guy, who smelled like heaven, who was one of the most handsome men I'd ever seen in real life, was into my design.

Still, all of that wasn't what had my skin buzzing. The little hairs on my arms were prickling being so near this guy. Not out of fear; it wasn't fear I felt around him. But my senses were on high alert, and I kept trying to dissect him to figure out why I felt this weirdness around him.

"You really sure about this?" I asked again. "You want my design on your skin forever? You can be honest with me. It won't hurt my feelings if you hate my artwork. I mean, most people just choose the stuff from the wall. And—"

I was following him down the hall, back to my station. But he stopped on a dime and turned to me. I nearly bumped into him. "Stop it. Stop doubting yourself. Stop questioning me."

He stared at me with these insanely fierce blue eyes. The seriousness in those eyes made my heart race like a stampede of wild horses. They were eyes that could make a girl drop to her knees if asked. I was certain of that. I bet this guy could have sex with whomever he damn well pleased. One look like that, and any girl would be his.

"You are talented. I want you to put your design on my skin." He stepped closer. His voice unwavering. I stared up at him feeling paralyzed. "Then after I leave, I want you to tear that paper in your hand to pieces. Don't put it in on the wall for anyone else to get. Don't post it on

Instagram for the world to copy. I want it to be only mine."

He was intense. My conundrum over who the hell this guy was suddenly multiplied by one thousand. The way he spoke. The way his chest moved in a slow, even rhythm as he breathed. Not to mention, the way his shirt fit over the lines of his muscular chest. All of it had me at his mercy.

Completely at his mercy.

He had an invisible tether tied straight to me. I nodded, unable to speak. Then he touched me. His hands went to my neck.

In the four years I'd been working here, I'd never had a customer touch me. Not like this. His comments about my safety earlier—I'd ignored them. I'd never felt unsafe here. My coworker Finn was huge, he'd be back any minute, and I felt certain he could protect me from anything.

But then again, this guy's sudden touch wasn't unwelcome. The opposite, actually.

He had his hands on my neck. They were warm, wonderful. One of his thumbs traced over my skin, sending shivers all through me, and I'd never wanted anything more. Yes, he could have squeezed those hands around my neck. And it's possible I wouldn't have been able to fight him off. But he didn't squeeze. He moved closer. He pressed his lips to mine.

My eyes fluttered closed just as he kissed me. This guy had the softest lips. The gentlest lips. I could barely believe a guy as beautiful as this man was kissing me. His kiss wasn't fast or greedy. It wasn't angry the way I'd felt anger in his words. He took his time. He moved in slow motion. Even when he deepened the kiss, and I tasted his tongue, he still moved carefully. Fuck, it was nice. It felt like he was savoring me. For minutes we stood there kissing and enjoying each other. The crush I'd had on him the moment he walked through the front door compounded exponentially. I felt like goo with this man.

Until he broke away, and I opened my eyes.

"That kiss was..." he started to say.

Incredible?

"Inappropriate," he finished, moving a step backward. "I'm sorry. I'm having a shit day. I shouldn't have done that. I promise it won't happen again." His words were harsh, direct, to the point. Almost as if he'd slapped me with them. A stark contrast to the perfect, soft kiss he'd just pressed on my lips.

Asshole.

"You shouldn't have," I agreed. "I have to go make a transfer for the drawing. Go lay down."

He nodded, walking away.

I stood there for a moment, breathing in and out, fuming. He was a stranger. He meant nothing to me. So why was I feeling so pissed off over that one small kiss? I could barely think straight, I was so mad at him over it. Maybe because he started it and then he immediately took it away.

"Damn him," I whispered. I went back down the hall to the transfer machine. I needed to copy the design I'd just drawn onto transfer paper. So I did that. When I returned to my station, the guy was still there. For a moment, I'd been thinking he might have left. He hadn't left though; he was lying on my chair on his stomach with his pants half down around his hips like before. He had his head buried in his arms, and he didn't look up as I came closer and sat down next to his side.

Rolling my eyes, so freaking annoyed with him, I got to work. I used alcohol to rub away the old design then I transferred the new design onto his skin. I was forced to speak to him again, only for a moment, as I asked him if the placement of his tattoo was right.

"It's good," he mumbled.

Seemed like we were both mad at each other over that kiss. Not long after that Finn returned. The thing with Finn was this: when I first started working here, we'd sort of dated. Our short relationship had consisted of one very boring dinner. Followed by one awkward-as-hell hookup, in the very chair this guy was now lying in, where we bumped heads a lot and the fluorescent lights killed the mood before we could even get to the good stuff. After that we gave up on trying to date and both decided we were meant to just be friends. We'd been good friends since. We even had this understanding between us, an act we would sometimes play, whenever one of us felt uncomfortable with a customer. Usually it was Finn who was the uncomfortable one, not me.

"Going okay?" Finn asked, stepping into my station to check on me. I could smell the onion and garlic on him from the pizza he must have just eaten.

"Fine, babe. It's going fine, babe."

"Love you, babe," he said to me, instantly understanding what I meant. He grabbed an extra chair from the corner and plopped it straight down next to my chair.

"Love you, too," I muttered in return.

That was it. That was our code with one another. The guy on the table—he didn't even so much as flinch over my fake 'I love you' exchange with Finn. He continued to lie perfectly still.

~ CHAPTER 3 ~

NICK

Jesus Christ, this was awkward. I kissed a girl with a boyfriend. *Meat Head* was her boyfriend. Of course he was. Why wouldn't he be? Because my shitty luck always worked that way. I always found myself in these impossible situations. To make things worse, *Boyfriend* had positioned himself right next to my head, acting like Amanda's own personal bodyguard. If I turned to look left, I would have been staring straight at his crotch. It was like the dude knew somehow what I'd done. He knew I'd kissed his girlfriend, and now he was hovering over me.

I lay still while Amanda worked on my tattoo. I said absolutely nothing the entire time. She could have been putting Bugs Bunny on my ass, and I wouldn't have opened my mouth.

An hour or two passed. No other customers entered the shop, so her bodyguard had no reason to move from his post. "I thought you were doing a different turtle," he asked her at one point. *Had it taken him a full hour to notice the difference?*

"We changed it," she answered.

"Did you draw that?"

"Yeah."

"Cool."

I thought her tattoo was better than cool. I mean, coming into the shop, my only criteria had been 'sea turtle.' So when she decided she didn't like the one I'd picked, I was open to a different design. But then she started sketching, and I'd honestly never seen anything like it.

None of the other pieces in the shop owner's portfolio wall were even close to what she'd drawn. She had a unique style. It was all sharp lines and open edges, purposely meant to look like a sketch. Then she drew sails morphing from the turtle's back. Something completely random. But it worked. It was, *really,* the coolest design. But her insecurity about it gave me the impression this woman didn't have the slightest idea how talented she really was. *Meat Head* certainly didn't get it.

"All done," she finally said.

It had been a little over two hours. Her bodyguard took a breath. He stood up and stepped away. He didn't go far. I could see his curly hair over the divider that separated Amanda's station from the next.

She peeled off her gloves. "Can I take a picture of it?"

"No social media posts," I reminded her.

"I know. I won't."

"Then I don't mind." If she wanted a picture of my ass, I wasn't going to stop her. Nah, in all seriousness, I got the impression she was relatively new at this. Maybe this was her first design taken only from her imagination, and she felt proud of her artwork—and rightfully so. She took the picture on her phone. Then she flipped it around for me to see.

I simply nodded. *I loved it.*

"I'm going to bandage it up now. Don't take the bandage off for twenty-four hours. I've got a paper with care instructions on it. You've got to follow them exactly. Otherwise you're risking an infection." Her pretty brown eyes flickered up to mine. I stood there next to her, so close to her, and I felt the heat between us again. I'd felt it in the hallway earlier. I'd kissed her because of that heat, and then immediately regretted it. For good reason, because it turned out she had a boyfriend. But mostly I regretted it because I wasn't in any sort of state to go around kissing random girls.

"You have to treat it like it's a wound because it is a wound." She touched her lips. It was so fucking fast, the slightest movement of her hand to those lush, pink lips. And something zapped through me. Was she still thinking about our kiss? Is that what that touch meant? Because now I sure as hell was.

There was a pause in the conversation before she suddenly asked, "Do you like it?" There was so much vulnerability in her words. She hadn't asked *Meat Head* if he liked it. Maybe she only was seeking out my approval because the ink was on my skin. But her question felt... like more than a question about the ink. It felt like she was trying to ask me something else.

"I do."

"Okay. Good. That's good." She bent over. She touched her hand to my skin. With it she rubbed on another thin layer of petroleum jelly over my new ink. Her fingers were cold, they moved slow. *Was it my imagination or did they linger?* I found myself nearly quaking under her gentle touch. I had to force myself to think about how long and painfully boring tomorrow's drive to Maine would be, about all the hours I'd spent dreading the inevitable, just to avoid going hard from her simple touch. After that, she covered the spot with a bandage and medical tape. She stood back up.

Her cheeks were a little flushed.

"All set. Meet me at the register."

She stepped away, allowing me a minute to get dressed, which consisted of just pulling up my pants over the bandage. I lingered for a minute, with my heart racing over this girl, a complete stranger. I studied her small space. Not much said it was hers. There was a mirror with an ornate frame. Some other framed art on the wall, lots of tattooing supplies, and one small picture on her work desk. Her and an older man. I assumed the man in the picture was her dad. They were standing on one of the piers in the area.

I stepped away, up to the front of the stop. There I paid. It was all business and pleasantries. But I felt sick to my stomach now. I didn't know why, I hardly knew a thing about this girl, but I didn't want to leave her.

Fuck.

I   didn't   know   what   to   do.

~ CHAPTER 4 ~

AMANDA

He paid. The end.

Then the bell chimed on the front door to *Kill Devil Ink,* and my mystery man disappeared outside into the rain. Gone forever. Bummer, too, because there was something about him, one of those 'can't-put-your-finger-on-it' sort of things, that made him different. But I told myself that 'difference' I felt was based solely on his looks. Nothing more. He wasn't special. Just handsome.

He paid, he left, and that was the end of it.

"What was that about?" Finn asked, interrupting my thoughts, drawing my eyes off the door. He leaned his muscular, tatted arms onto the counter, staring up at me like he genuinely cared. Finn *did* care. He was always looking out for me.

"I don't know. We kissed while you were gone. It just sort of happened."

"What?" His eyes narrowed. "He kissed *you?* Or you kissed him?"

"Him—me. But it was reciprocated."

"So, why'd you use the code word?" *'Babe,'* specifically, was our code word. The *'I love you'* exchange was more of a confirmation that the word had been purposefully used.

"I don't know." I avoided eye contact with Finn now, staring down at the receipt I'd received back from the turtle guy instead. *Holy shit, he'd left me a tip double the amount of his tattoo.* Wow. In four years, I'd never been given a tip like this. Most people gave around ten percent, not two hundred percent.

I entered the number into the cash register.

Well, silver-lining, I guess.

"I don't want to talk about it," I muttered.

"Yeah. Okay. I get it."

Did he get it? He stepped away, not asking anymore questions.

For another half hour, Finn and I killed time. I cleaned my station, set up for a client I had scheduled tomorrow, and then hung around Finn's station while he did the same.

"Let's close early," he suggested. "No one else is coming."

I nodded. These weeknights in the off-season, when tourism in the Outer Banks was at its lowest, were always dull. We were just wasting time and electricity being here any longer.

"I'm going to call John; tell him we're closing early. Then I'll call Julie to come get me." Julie was Finn's current girlfriend. He always had a new one, and they never lasted longer than a month. Julie was about the same as the rest of them: blonde, high-pitched voice, trying-too-hard. Her expiration date had to be coming soon.

"I'll get my stuff." I went back to my station, double-checking everything one last time, when I noticed something on the ground. It was a gray, knit hat. I'd only had two clients tonight. I didn't remember either one wearing a hat. I picked it up, running my fingers over the material. It looked homemade, and well loved. *Did it belong to turtle guy?* I put it in my purse. I don't know why—we had a lost-and-found in the shop—but I took it anyway. Maybe I wanted to keep a piece of my mystery guy.

It wasn't long before Julie showed. She lay on her horn, honking to let Finn know she was here. "You go ahead," I decided last second. "I think I'm going to stick around a little longer, try out some different sketches." I shrugged. I could sketch at home, but something inside me urged me to stay.

"You sure? I could stay a little longer too. Julie wouldn't mind coming inside and hanging with us. She likes you."

I had to hide a smile. No way in hell did Julie want to come inside and hang out with me. I was fairly sure she despised me. "No, that's okay. I'm good. Go on ahead. I'll be fine."

"Okay. Turn the front lights off after I go. Don't let anyone else in tonight. And don't stay too late."

"I'm fine," I repeat. "Have a good night."

Why do boys assume we are all damsels in distress? First turtle guy did it with his comments about Finn leaving me alone with a customer. Now it felt like Finn was doing something similar.

Finn gave me a quick hug before he disappeared out the door and into the rain. I sat down at the counter. I started sketching an alternative version of the tattoo I already had planned for a customer coming in tomorrow. I used the same style I'd used with the turtle. Lots of open lines and shading. It was meant to look like someone had sketched it straight onto the skin. Maybe this new style I'd dreamed up—maybe I was on to something. Maybe it could be my trademark, almost like a signature. A lot of artists have signature styles. Maybe this could be mine.

I'd only just begun when I heard a noise. The bell on the front door chimed. I'd forgotten to lock up after Finn left just minutes ago. I hadn't turned off the front light either. "We're closed..." I started to say. But I shut my mouth the moment I saw it was turtle tattoo guy. Back again.

This man, stepping in through the front door... holy hell. I mean, this guy was the type of man who could have had long hair, short hair, beard, no beard, *hell, a mustache,* and he'd be just as insanely handsome no matter what he did to himself. I set my pencil down. He was classically handsome—strong jawline, pretty blue eyes, masculinity oozing out of his pores. But it was something else he had that made him different.

Charisma.

I finally put my finger on it. It was charisma. An almost permanent little smirk on his full lips. A confidence that shined in his bright blue eyes. A knowledge that he could probably get away with whatever the fuck he wanted, and it showed in that small smile. I didn't really question why he was back. It wasn't the hat. Something that worn and old—it wasn't his. No, he was back to finish what he'd started with me. And he didn't give a damn about Finn. Boundaries didn't matter to him. He could have me, he knew that, and he was here for that one thing.

~ CHAPTER 5 ~

NICK

My hat. *Fuck, my hat!* I'd left the tattoo shop, gotten on the road, deciding I'd just start driving straight for Maine tonight—why wait another day?— when I realized I didn't have my hat. Then I remembered that I'd had it in my hands when I'd first stepped into *Kill Devil Ink*. Somewhere in between first speaking with the girl named Amanda, showing her my ass, kissing her in the hallway, and leaving her with a couple hundred dollars from my bank account, I'd set it down somewhere. Hopefully my favorite hat was still there.

I turned my car around and headed back.

For the hat, not the girl.

I pulled into the parking lot, lingered in my car for a minute, debating with myself. I mean, it was just a stupid hat. It wasn't normal to be this attached to an inanimate object like a hat. But that hat was so much a part of me. I understood how crazy that made me, and yet, I still couldn't walk away from the stupid hat I'd had over half my life.

So I stepped out of my car into the dark, cold rain, wishing the hat were already on my head, ready to book it in and out of the shop, when I noticed the guy. What was his name? Meat Head. He raced through the rain, jogging toward a black Jeep waiting a few spots away from the door. Inside the Jeep, illuminated by the interior light, was a woman.

Meat Head climbed inside.

He kissed her.

He dug his hands in her (not pink) hair, he pressed his body to her body, and for a good minute I thought he was about to start humping her. Gross. But they broke apart and the light faded out. After that, the Jeep pulled away, speeding, splashing me with a huge wave of water from a puddle.

So he wasn't Amanda's boyfriend?

Interesting.

Very interesting.

I might have been annoyed, soaking wet and all, but I wasn't all that bothered by it. I went for the door instead. Amanda hadn't left; I could see her through the front windows, sitting at the counter drawing. Her eyes were intent on her work. And I swear to God, it felt like I didn't have full control over my feet.

They moved toward her. They walked inside the building. The bell on the front door chimed with my arrival. Her eyes moved to mine, and I realized coming back might not have been the best decision. She had my hat; it sat on the counter by her fingertips. But I wasn't looking at the hat. I was lost in her eyes. And a little trapped in the thick air that seemed to be surrounding us.

"You're soaking wet," she muttered. "We have some towels in the back." She swiveled in her chair, hopping up, hurrying away.

I let out a breath, running my hands through my hair, scolding myself for being back here. My hat was still on the counter. *Grab it. Run away. Leave before she returns.* That was what my brain told me to do, but my feet didn't do a damn thing to comply. Suddenly she was back, standing in front of me, handing me a dark purple towel.

I took it. I wiped my face with it. But mostly I was waiting to see what would happen. Why I felt like I couldn't move. Why I felt like the room was closing in around us. Why I had such an undeniable attraction to this woman, her pink hair, and the ink on her skin. It was annoying that I didn't have it in me to just grab my hat and get the hell out of there, distance myself from her.

"You overpaid for your tattoo," she muttered, a hint of irritation in her voice. "Most people tip between ten or twenty. Or nothing. You tipped something like two hundred percent. Why?"

"It doesn't matter."

"No, it does."

"I don't know. I liked your work."

She moved her hands to her hips. She had the nicest body. A little thinner than some of the Maine women I'd grown up with. But the small curves she did have nearly gave me goosebumps. "You couldn't have liked it *that* much."

"No, really, I like it *that* much."

"You're full of shit."

"At least I'm not making up fake boyfriends."

Her eyes narrowed, further proving what I already assumed. Meat Head wasn't really her boyfriend. I wasn't sure what he was to her, probably only a friend, but I knew now that their weird *'I love you'* exchange had been some kind of show—for me.

"At least I don't have a permanent turtle on my ass," she shot back at me.

She was playing with me, I realized. It got me to smile. She gave me a look like she dared me to say something else. Instantly, I let down my guard. *You win, sweetheart.* I knew the turtle in that place was silly. But I liked it. Something behind her eyes told me she liked it too. No... she loved it. Something told me—maybe it was the pounding in my own chest—if I wanted, I could have this girl. Right now. Right here. That idea made it impossible to keep a level head. It made my cock go hard, *so fucking hard.* She made my skin feel tight. She made my fingertips burn. She made me itch with a need I hadn't felt in a while. She made me forget all the shit in my life.

I kissed her.

For the second time tonight, without control, I kissed this woman whom I barely knew.

~ CHAPTER 6 ~

AMANDA

Blame it on the rain. Come tomorrow, or maybe fifteen minutes from now when I came to my senses, that would be my excuse—the rain. The sound outside the windows, the smell it gave the air, and the way this man looked soaking wet. *Blame it on the rain.* His lips were on my lips again, which I did nothing to stop, and it was completely and totally, one hundred percent the rain's fault.

His wet shirt clung to his chest, to every line of his washboard abs, and it made me want to drop my mouth open and drool. He walked in, not bothered by anything at all. I don't even know how it happened. But one second he was pushing my buttons, arguing with me, and the next he was pushing his lips against mine. That was how smooth this guy was. And dammit, if I didn't fall for his charm in less than thirty seconds all over again.

This time was different than our first kiss in the hallway. Maybe because I knew, and he knew, Finn wasn't coming back. It felt dangerous, reckless, out of control, stupid. I didn't do this sort of thing with clients. Or any stranger, for that matter.

Danger be damned though, because I ran my hands over his wet shirt, feeling the heat of his body underneath. I touched his strong neck. This guy oozed masculinity like he ate it for breakfast. I felt his skin there before I dug my fingers into his short hair.

That was when he pulled back.

He broke the kiss. For a moment, I thought I'd done something wrong. I thought he was about to leave again. My heart sank to the floor because of it. But that wasn't what happened at all.

"Tonight's my last night in town. I'm leaving for good in the morning. Nothing's going to change that. But..." He breathed out. His blue eyes lifted to mine. "But I wouldn't mind spending my one last night with you."

I swallowed.

"Amanda," he said softly. "Spend the night with me."

I let out a choked, giddy little laugh. *He knew my name.* The way he asked... nothing had ever felt better. How was this happening? This *freaking* gorgeous, straight-laced, put-together man shows up out of nowhere, interested in me. Did I dream him up out of thin air? Did I draw him into existence like one of my tattoos? Any second now, I was going to wake up, and all of this will have been a dream.

I stepped away from him. I went to the front door, locking it from the inside. I found the light switch which controlled the exterior front lights and the neon sign. I flipped it off. I flipped off the inside light, too. It dimmed everything. It signaled to him he could stay. And boy did he read that signal loud and clear. He tugged at his wet shirt, peeling it off over his head before letting it drop. It slapped the ground. *Holy crap.* He looked so good without a shirt. I barely got a chance to look before my Mystery Man returned to me, backing me against the counter where I'd been drawing before. He tugged my shirt off as well, dragging his fingers against my skin, leaving me in only the cotton bra I'd picked out this morning.

He kissed me again as he unbuckled his belt and his jeans. "Say no, Amanda. Tell me to stop."

I said nothing. Which led him to push down his jeans. They fell to his ankles with their heavy, wet weight. He began working to get his shoes off and his mouth never left mine. His hands were on my skin now, touching and exploring. He pulled down the fabric of my bra, exposing my chest to him and the room. Next thing I knew he had his mouth on one of my nipples. He dragged his tongue over my sensitive flesh.

I caught my breath in my throat.

"Fuck, Amanda, tell me to stop."

His eyes caught mine. It had been several moments since he'd looked directly at me. Electricity moved through me—something powerful—at just that one look.

"I won't tell you to stop," I whispered. I don't even know why he kept asking me to, what it meant. He was in control, not me, so if he wanted this to stop, he could go ahead and stop it already. But in truth, I knew neither of us wanted this to stop.

A smile, so slight, touched his lips. It was hands down the sexiest thing I'd ever seen in my life. He didn't speak again after that. He worked at getting the rest of my clothes off, the rest of his off. Then he had me up on the counter, his mouth between my legs.

The world was spinning.

I didn't stand a chance. I never did. Not once throughout any of this. I think that was why I'd pulled the *'I love you'* thing with Finn earlier when he was here, made Finn sit between me and this guy while I did his tattoo, because even then I knew I needed a bodyguard of sorts to protect me from this man.

His mouth moved in a slow, torturous motion. I felt myself building rapidly toward the inevitable. Who was he? Just a stranger passing through town. Just some guy I'd never see again after tonight. His hands ran up my thighs. He pushed my legs wider apart. He kept moving his mouth against me. My brain stopped overanalyzing, for a few glorious seconds, and the world melted away.

Sweet bliss hit me. It spread through my body, across my chest, and up my neck. It was pure heaven. The guy knew what he'd done. Because after he moved to kiss me, pressing his lips with my taste on them against my mouth. He let out a noise, a satisfied little hint of a laugh, before he touched gently the spot between my legs. I was wet and still hypersensitive.

"What next?" he asked.

"How about you tell me your name?" I whispered.

~ CHAPTER 7 ~

NICK

All night long, I played with Amanda. I'd never had a night quite like this—one that felt so free and effortless. Considering my ex-girlfriend Emma had been a virgin, had remained a virgin throughout the course of our six-month relationship, and never once did anything physical with me, this felt like a strange contrast.

It was overdue.

And amazing.

We didn't have sex until the next morning—the sun was close to rising. I hadn't told her my name all night long despite her asking for it a couple times. I'd avoided it because of Emma. I'd realized I knew who John was: He owned this shop. Emma knew John. Emma had mentioned his name once or twice while we'd dated. I figured John was likely Amanda's boss. I don't know if Amanda knew Emma or not. Maybe there were a couple degrees of separation between the two girls; maybe not. Either way, since I was leaving town after all this, I figured it was better if Amanda didn't know my name.

I came inside her.

A night of foreplay, of messing around without going all the way, and something about the imminent morning pushed me to cross the finish line. Something about the idea of never seeing Amanda again. About this being my only chance to be with her. I was still raw from my breakup with Emma. If I were being honest with myself, still emotional and angry and hurt. But this girl… she wasn't Emma.

I fucking loved that she wasn't Emma. That she let me inside her. That she moved with me, matched me, let her guard down completely while I fucked her. Hell, that she even let me fuck her at all. It was a stark difference from my time with Emma. And it was what turned this into so much more.

"Tell me your name," she cried out. Amanda was still after that one little detail.

I was on top of her, thrusting deeper and harder with every push inside her, losing all my control. I smiled, kissing her, pressing my sweaty forehead to hers.

"No way, sweetheart," I breathed.

She'd be sore tomorrow from the wild way we were screwing.

I loved knowing that.

"My name doesn't matter."

I kept pumping.

She had to be close to coming.

"Damn you," she whispered. Her mouth dropped open. Her eyes closed. She dug her nails into my forearms. "I hate you."

I knew she didn't.

"You're an asshole."

I knew she didn't think so.

She cried out, finally falling over that edge this final time. Seeing her come while I was buried deep inside her, her nipples hard little peaks, her bare skin and all its ink on display just for me, her pink hair, wild all around her head, made me explode deep inside her.

Nothing had ever felt this good.

Or been this easy.

Or felt this right.

I pulled out and I couldn't stop smiling at her, with her, mesmerized that after everything with Emma, I'd wound up having such an amazing night. Maybe I wasn't as broken as I thought. Maybe there was hope for me yet. Light at the end of what had felt like the longest, darkest tunnel. I let out a sigh, one of content, and was about to pull Amanda closer. I wanted to hold her. I wanted to tell her how much this night had meant to me. Except our time was cut short when the bell on the front door chimed.

I thought with certainty she'd locked it last night.

I guess not. Or maybe the person who entered had a key.

It was John. The owner. *He'd used a key.*

John's skin was a canvas for the all the artwork he'd accrued over his lifetime. He was in his thirties. The kind of guy who seemed like he knew exactly who he was and didn't give a fuck what anyone else thought of him. "Wow," he said, seeing us both naked and in an overly precarious position. He covered his eyes with one of his hands immediately.

"Holy shit," Amanda whispered. She climbed away from me and began scrambling to get dressed. The easy smile I'd put on her lips disappeared in a second.

I wasn't all that embarrassed. John seemed more embarrassed than me. "Not exactly how I wanted to start my morning," he grumbled.

"I know. I'm so sorry, John."

"I have rules about having sex on those couches. I told you them when you first started working here, didn't I?"

"Yeah. You did."

Amanda pulled on her jeans. Then, suddenly, she had on her bra, her shirt, even her shoes, before I had stood up from the couch. She tossed my shirt at me, still damp, shoved my pants into my arms, and gave me a look like I was the enemy.

Or maybe that look was fear.

Was this my cue to leave?

Suddenly I felt sick to my stomach. I wasn't sure I wanted to leave. My car was packed to the brim with all my belongings, ready for my move back home. My parents were expecting me later tomorrow after my twelve hour drive up the coast. I'd even promised my friend Lou I'd see her first thing this Friday. But Amanda... I don't know, part of me wasn't in that big of a hurry to leave her.

"Is it safe for me to open my eyes yet?" John asked, still hanging out awkwardly next to the front door with his tattooed fingers over his eyes. He seemed like a decent guy. I bet he really did have them covered.

I pulled on my pants and shirt.

Amanda looked upset. Whether it was with me or the situation, I didn't know for sure. "You can open them," she announced now that I was also fully dressed.

"Alright," John said. He removed his hand from his face. "Let's pretend like this never happened. And don't let it happen again. I mean it." He walked deeper into his shop. He passed us without making eye contact, before he disappeared down the hallway.

"You should go," Amanda muttered. She looked ashamed. I wasn't ashamed at all. Or worried about what John Michaels thought of me. Then again, if John had recognized me, if he knew I used to date Emma, which he probably did, it was only a matter of time before Amanda learned who I was.

"Yep," I said to her. "Thanks for last night, Amanda."

She couldn't even look me in the eyes, but I kissed her on the cheek anyway. She flinched a little at my touch. Did she regret everything? Because I regretted nothing.

"It was the best," I muttered. "And I really mean that."

I walked for the door. A lot of the sadness and emotions I still felt from my breakup with Emma came flooding back. Almost like my heart was splintering open for the second time. Only this time, it wasn't Emma doing it to me. "My name is Nick," I said, in case anyone was listening, pushing open the door, letting the cold morning air inside.

The sky on the other side was a striking painting of pinks and oranges as the sun had started to show. Right this moment though, I would have preferred last night's monsoon.

"Nick Jasmine," I added. And then I walked out the door.

~ CHAPTER 8 ~

AMANDA

I was mortified. John Michaels was this no-nonsense kind of a guy. He came to work, he did his job, and nobody fucked with him. Now I was always going to be the girl he caught buck-ass naked on his precious leather couches in the waiting area of *his shop*.

Seriously, he loved those couches. They were this tan leather that he'd drawn, or maybe burned, his designs into. More than the ink on his skin, they showed just how talented he was. Since the moment I started working here, I'd looked up to John. I wanted to be him. Now he probably thought the worst of me.

For the rest of the day, I kept to myself. I tore up the drawings I'd been working on before Nick came back last night. The one of another tattoo idea I'd intended to present to my first client today. It had been the same style as Nick's turtle.

Speaking of Nick. He'd said his name just before he left, and I had a pretty good idea who he was now. Emma Winchester, a friend, had been dating a guy named Nick. An out-of-towner. She had a new boyfriend now, but the guy she'd previously been seeing was a marine biologist, who would bore her to death with his stories about dolphins... and sea turtles. That explained a lot. She told me once that he was so boring, she literally fell asleep during a sit-down dinner with him. No wonder Nick had been a man of so few words last night.

Sex with him had been good. More than good—fucking amazing. But between John catching us, and learning Nick was my friend's ex-boyfriend, I was pretty glad he'd walked away.

Later that day, as the sun was beginning to set, I stepped up to the railing at the end of the pier, staring down into the greenish-gray waves below. "Hi, Bobby," I breathed, "how's the catch today?"

"I caught four so far."

He had. I saw the fish he'd caught lying there, flapping out their last little bit of life next to his cooler a few feet away from his feet. Four was decent.

"Where's your pole?" he asked me.

Bobby was my father's friend. All my life, since before I could walk, my Daddy brought me out to this pier. He loved it. He'd spend hours here. His whole life always revolved around the next fish on his line. We ate fish for dinner eight nights out of seven each week. What we didn't eat, my father would sell. His obsession with the sea and the fish was the whole reason Mom left us years back. Now Daddy was gone too. It was just Bobby I had left. Other regulars would come and go. Some men I'd known my whole life just like Bobby. But without fail, no matter the weather, Bobby could always be found at the end of this pier each and every evening. Just like my old man.

"I screwed up at work today," I muttered. I came tonight not to fish but for some connection to my dad. "Big time. I thought about quitting all day."

"You show me a man who ain't screwed up before at work. I'll show you a liar. It's okay, 'Manda, we all screw up."

"It was so embarrassing though."

"The sea don't care what happens. You come here. You see how big she is. And you know you're small."

"Are you saying we're all insignificant?" I asked him.

"I'm saying life's too short to worry about what other people think of you." Well, he had a point there. "Here," he said to me. "Take my line for a minute. There ain't nothing a fish on the end of your line can't fix."

It was fishing, not an ice-cold beer. But for Bobby, for my dad, that was the simple truth. Coming out to the ocean, standing on the end of this pier, feeling the breeze, watching the waves, holding a pole with bait on the end of the line—it could help heal anything.

It put today in perspective, almost instantly.

I had a really good night last night with this really handsome stranger. A man who, in my opinion, didn't seem boring at all, who treated me nicely, who smelled like heaven, and who must be passionate enough about sea turtles to get one permanently on his ass.☐

I smiled, thinking about his tattoo, shaking my head. Then I wished that I might get to see him again one day. That I might get a second chance with him. Because I'd let him walk away and something told me I shouldn't have.

~ CHAPTER 9 ~

NICK

Twelve hours in the car and one night sleeping in a questionable motel—here I was. The wind in my face, standing on the top deck as I rode the last ferry of the day from Portland to Peaks Island. It was freezing this time of year in Maine. I should have stayed with my car on the lower deck. But since it had been nearly a year since I'd last been home, watching the island grow closer and closer from the vacant top deck of this boat was sort of a 'welcome home' ritual.

As I stared down the harsh wind, I realized... *damn, I forgot my hat.*

I'd forgotten it on the counter at *Kill Devil Ink*; For a second time, I'd carelessly left it behind. I'd probably never seen that hat again. Losing it stung. That hat once belonged to my late grandfather. Something I found in his attic after his death. One of the only possessions I had that linked me to him. It was something I'd worn continuously throughout my late childhood, into my teens, even in college. If my house, if I ever owned a house, were on fire it would have been at the top of my list of things to save. Only more recently I'd become better about not wearing it nearly every day of my life. But knowing it might be gone forever weighed on me.

The ferry finished its approach toward Peaks Island. I left my bitter cold post on the top deck, returned to the lower deck, and climbed into my car. I started the engine, taking a breath, closing my eyes for the last couple seconds of freedom.

Welcome home, Nick.

"**Mom!**" I called out. The gate to the driveway had been left open, the front door unlocked, the lights in the foyer all turned on, but I yelled into an empty house. It smelled like something had been baking. When I went into the empty kitchen, I even opened the oven, peaking inside. Nothing. But it was still warm.

Where was everyone?

"I'm supposed to tell you to go find them out back," said a small voice. One I knew very well, but it was a voice I'd never heard inside this house.

I caught my breath and turned around. It was Lou; my best friend in this world. *Holy shit!* Standing. Breathing. Looking relatively normal, in normal clothes that I was willing to bet my mother had bought for her. Despite how much of today I'd spent with only depression running through me, I smiled at my best friend. It was surreal to be seeing her anywhere outside the library she called her home.

"It's a long story," she whispered, catching my confused expression.

This was amazing. "I have nothing but time."

From the looks of it, she'd even been showering regularly. I'd only ever seen her hair greasy and matted to her head. Today her hair looked washed. "You don't, actually," she whispered. "There's a welcome home party waiting for you. See the tent?" She nodded at the window.

Sure enough. I saw the tent outside, like a wedding tent, and about a million cars parked in the grass around the outside.

I cringed.

"It's supposed to be a surprise," Lou told me. "So, surprise!"

Oh God, my mom knew no limits. I should have expected this. I didn't care about some party, where all the people in attendance were either my parents' friends or my brother Mick's baseball connections.

"I'm more surprised to see you here. Healthy. Outside the library."

"The library's having renovations. I was forced to leave. I had nowhere else to go."

"You should have told me this." We communicated through emails. She used to use the computer at the library. Now what was she using? My mom's? The old one in my room?

"I guess I wanted to surprise you, too. I'm going back upstairs. Have fun at your party. It's great to see you, Nick."

I would have hugged her. But I'd never hugged her once since we'd been friends. She needed people to keep a few feet of distance, which I'd always respected. Lou was like a sister to me. She had her phobias; phobias I still, to this day, didn't fully understand. But what made us friends was that she was the only person who understood, accepted, and respected my own phobias in return.

Lou went upstairs. I knew all of this had to be hard on her. And I'd try to talk it out with her later. But for now, I needed to go deal with my family. Fortunately, or maybe unfortunately, I was good at something Lou wasn't good at: I could put on a mask when I wanted, a smile on my face, a spring in my step, an easiness in my voice, and I could approach the world. I could trick others into believing I was relatively normal. Charming even. I did it so well, I'd easily slept with my pink-haired girl two nights ago. Though, truth be told, I wasn't entirely sure how much of my time with Amanda had been me acting verses me just being me.

Tonight was one hundred and ten percent acting. I headed outside to the party, I put on that same fucking smile, and I approached the world. I just wished I had my damn hat.

~ CHAPTER 10 ~

AMANDA

"Another person wants one of your sketch tattoos." John announced, stepping into my station. "She drove four hours just for you, halfway across the state. She said she found you on Instagram. She's practically freaking out in the waiting area."

"Okay," I answered. "That's good, right?"

"That's great, Amanda. Really great."

I gave him a small smile. "Could you give me a couple minutes before you send her back? I just need to use the bathroom really quickly."

"Sure thing."

John walked off.

Since my embarrassing little 'incident' where John caught me buck naked with a man between my legs, not once had he brought it up. *Thank God!* In fact, John was so good at ignoring it, that it was almost as if it never happened.

Finn, who I'd confessed to a few days after the 'incident,' knew too. I'd found it impossible to keep it all to myself. Finn teased me about it for almost two weeks. I think it gave him something to talk about, a distraction, since he'd broken up with Julie that same night. Strangely though, Finn had yet to find a Julie replacement. Or at least, not one I knew of.

But even Finn had stopped talking about the incident. It had been almost six weeks now. By this point nobody cared or, hopefully, remembered. Only, I did. I still had the guy's ugly old beanie sitting on my desk. It was a knit hat that should be in the lost-and-found box, but instead remained on my desk. I knew it was his because the inside tag had the name 'Nick' written on it. It was faded and worn, but still legible.

I kept wondering if Nick came back later that night, all soaking wet from the rain, only for the hat. What if he hadn't come back for me at all? What if our time together had been more of an afterthought on his part that meant nothing?

I stepped away from my station, down the hall, and slipped into the bathroom. My heart was racing like mad, practically giving me chest palpitations, because I had something more important to do right now than any tattoo.

From the back pocket of my jean skirt, I pulled out the pregnancy test I'd stashed there earlier. I'd picked it up from the pharmacy on my lunch break. I'd picked it up because it had been enough time since my night with Nick and I had yet to get my period.

We were stupid. We hadn't used a condom. I was on birth control, at the time, but I'd been horrible the past month about taking my pill regularly. That night with Nick was just so unexpected. I hadn't had sex with anyone in months, so taking my pill regularly wasn't at the top of my priority list. Now here I was, peeing on a stick, wondering what the hell I'd do if the test came back positive.

I finished using the bathroom, put the lid on the test, set it on the sink, and set a timer on my phone.

Three minutes.

Three fucking minutes.

It felt like an eternity.

I squealed when, suddenly, the door to the bathroom opened.

"Hello! I'm in here!" I yelled at the intruder.

It was Finn.

"I'm sorry. So sorry—" He looked mortified for having barged in on me in the bathroom. But then he paused. He didn't move to leave the bathroom. He must have seen the test on the sink because he asked, "What the hell is that?"

Perfect. "Nothing," I tried to lie.

"That doesn't look like nothing." He quickly opened the door wider, squeezed himself into the bathroom, which was no bigger than a closet, and closed the door behind him. "Seriously?" he asked, looking at me like he'd never been more shocked by anything in his life. "Turtle-ass guy? No fucking way?"

I closed my eyes, breathing in through my nose. "Yeah, I'm aware of how stupid this is. But, yes, turtle-ass guy!"

"What's it say?"

"I don't know yet!"

"Are you gonna keep it?"

"I don't even know *yet* if I have to make that decision!"

"Well freaking look! The suspense is killing me!"

"Killing you?!" I breathed, reaching for the test. "Think how I feel!" I accidentally bumped it with my arm and the test flew across the room, hitting the tile floor. It was impossibly small in the bathroom. I bent over, looking for it, when someone else opened the door.

It was John this time.

"Jesus Christ!" He shielded his blue eyes with his tattooed knuckles. "Not again!"

I understood how this looked... me down on my knees. Finn, who slept with everyone, standing there, looking guilty as hell. But whatever John assumed we were doing, wasn't what was happening at all. "It's not what you think," I muttered.

I found the test. I stood back up to my feet. John uncovered his eyes. He saw what was in my hand. He saw I wasn't doing anything with Finn, that we were both fully clothed. But now John knew I might be pregnant too. The more the merrier, I guess. Whatever.

I read the test.

Fuckity-fuck.

Positive.

"Whose?" John asked. "Sorry," he quickly corrected. "It's not my business. I shouldn't have asked that."

Well, it was about to be all my colleagues' business. I was pregnant. Maybe I didn't look so pregnant right this moment. But they'd all know in a couple months when my stomach grew, so what did it matter? I felt defeated. That night, that *mistake*, was turning cruddier and cruddier.

"The turtle guy. Nick or whatever his name was." I remembered his name perfectly fine even if I acted like I didn't. "But for now, both of you, please swear to me you won't tell anyone."

Both guys agreed.

Huffing under my breath, pretending like I was merely inconvenienced by all this, I left the bathroom. Off to start my eighth tattoo in my new 'sketch' style. People had been starting to request these specific tattoos from me. This sort of attention at work—it was unusual and unexpected. It was always John's work people came for. Never mine.

I tried to keep breathing steadily as I spoke with the girl who had driven four hours to see me. I tried to keep my hands from shaking. I tried to focus on her, and not on my stomach. But my stomach, or more accurately my uterus, soon became all I could think about. Underneath the surface of my skin—*inside me!*—there was a little life beginning to take shape and form.

Holy shit.

I almost felt excited. I don't why. This wasn't a good thing. But some small piece of me liked the idea of having a baby. Weirder still—I think I liked the idea of having Nick's baby. I mean, the man was gorgeous. Imagine what his kids might look like. For six weeks now, I'd been thinking our night together meant absolutely nothing. He didn't come back for me. He didn't call the shop, not even about his lost hat. He probably forgot about me the moment he walked away.

But having *his* baby. I kind of liked the idea of it. I wouldn't track him down or anything. At least not anytime soon. But for a small fleeting moment, I liked that I had this little piece of him with me.

The moment lasted only a second.

The next thought was pure hatred for the man.

~ CHAPTER 11 ~

NICK

Lou lived in my parent's attic. I guess it was a small upgrade from the attic of the old library down the street from my brother's house. Lou had agoraphobia. Which meant she was basically afraid of everything—stepping outside, being around people, experiencing the unknown.

I met her years ago, in middle school, when I'd been working on this project with some of my classmates at the same old library where she lived.

My whole life, at that point in time, was this huge charade of fitting in. It was important for me to act like the other kids at my private school, talk like them and behave like them. We all came from money. We all exuded confidence. We all excelled at sports, at school, at life. Basically, I was an adult in a kid's body. That year I lost my grandfather and gained a brother.

My brother, who came from a trailer park, who was my father's bastard son from some random hookup that happened long before he even met my mom, was suddenly in my life. I don't know how Mick did it—*yes, his name is Mick, coincidence*—but he came into our lives and was perfect.

Mick looked the part, acted the part, and was insanely good at baseball when I seemed to have been born with two left feet. And he didn't even seem phased by the sudden change. In fact, unlike me, I doubt he was acting at all. Basically, my new half-brother was the better version of myself.

Something happened during that group project. Out of nowhere, this tightness in my chest started. I felt a constriction in my lungs. I was dying. Literally *dying*. Or maybe having a heart attack. I didn't want to draw attention, so I slipped away from the group and snuck up the stairs that led into the dome of this old library. There was a warning sign and a chain I shouldn't have crossed, but I did it anyway, and I moved up the stairs, higher and higher. At the top level, between two very tall shelves of books, I lay on the floor.

I couldn't breathe.

I couldn't see—but maybe that was from all the tears in my eyes.

I felt pathetic.

I felt like a coward.

I felt a little like jumping from the top level of that tall dome. I hated the world. I hated my new, perfect, trailer-park brother. I hated that my grandfather had been taken way before his time.

I didn't jump. I didn't move. Eventually the feeling dissipated. The worst of it passed. I noticed a small girl there with me, looking at me from the floor. She looked homeless. Her clothes were dirty and worn and two sizes too big for her. "I have panic attacks sometimes too," she whispered.

I might have been terrified by her; maybe thought she was a ghost at first. But she had the kindest eyes.

That was the start of our friendship. I'd been coming to Lou with my problems ever since. One of the librarians at the library took care of Lou, allowed her to live there. But with the new renovations, Lou had been forced to leave and face the world. At twenty-three, same age as me, she'd left for the first time in almost ten years.

Trust me, in the past I'd tried many times to get her to leave, live with us, go to school. She never would. I still couldn't believe she was in my house. It was the craziest thing.

"You're miserable here," she said to me today at breakfast time. Well, maybe it was past one in the afternoon, but breakfast time for me since I'd just gotten up for the day. My parents were long gone—at work or out shopping, whatever it was they normally did on a Friday morning.

"What? I'm fine," I said through a giant bite of cereal. I slurped milk everywhere, trying to act like she hadn't just pegged me down in a second flat.

"You're not fine. You're back to being you. Being all fake and weird and sleeping all the time. Only, you're minus your hat."

I swallowed. I still missed my hat. In some ways, that hat had been my guard against the world. When I wore it, I could be whomever I wanted.

"I heard you last night."

Fuck. I'd had a panic attack of my own last night. Mine were random, I think, coming on mostly without warning. Lou's were always triggered. I guess she'd heard me. Heard all the heavy breathing. It only lasted a few minutes, but those few minutes had been hell. At least, it hadn't been a nightmare. When I was younger, I had those too. Now it was just the occasional, debilitating, horrifying, panic attack.

"I'm okay," I lied.

"You told me—you said they weren't happening in North Carolina." Lou sat beside me, her elbows on the table. "Was that a lie?"

"No. Mine were better there." *Not really. Especially after Emma dumped me.*

"You told me you loved your job. That you loved the people there. That it was nothing like here. No pressure there. Nick, why are you back?"

Tears burned in my eyes. "It didn't work out with Emma. Everywhere I went, I kept running into her or her friends or someone she's connected to." Hell, even Amanda, and that one tiny, great second of time with the pink-haired girl—even that too had its connection to Emma.

Lou took a breath, giving me a look, pursing her lips. She seemed angry with me, but still managed to seem pure and innocent. "You said, when I was ready, I could come live with you. I could take that step and leave Maine, too."

I had said that. I'd said that to her a million times over. Throughout college. When I first got the job in North Carolina. I was constantly suggesting it. That offer was always on the table.

"But up until recently, Lou, you couldn't even leave the library. What changed?"

"I'm ready now. Something inside me is different. I left the library. Your mom helped me do it. She even took me shopping once. I did it. I got in her car, and I rode to the store. We went at six in the morning, she arranged it with the manager, and we went before anyone else was there. It was amazing. So I think I'm ready. I think I'm ready to start doing more. I want to go to North Carolina."

I think she was viewing North Carolina as this magical, mystical place. Where anything was possible. Where the birds sang, the sun shined, and the waves crashed upon the beach. But newsflash: Maine had just as many birds, just as much sunshine, excellent beaches. So there was clearly nothing magical about it. North Carolina was just far from my family. And despite my issues, I really loved my family. Especially my brother Mick. Turned out, he wasn't as bad I used to think he was at thirteen.

"What are you asking?"

"I'm asking you to take me to North Carolina. I'm asking you to get your rental house back and try again. To get your animal job back."

"Marine Biologist. Sea Turtle Specialist."

"That's the one. You love those turtles. They don't have turtles in Maine. Those little guys need you."

I stared at my soggy cereal. She had a point—they didn't have sea turtles here. Or jobs as exceptional as my job there. I'd moved to North Carolina for that specific job.

"They've probably already filled my position."

"But you could call and see if they haven't."

"I could."

"C'mon on, Nick. You were happy there. Happy before you met Emma. I'm sorry it didn't work out and she left you for some silly Rockstar." She had. Emma had literally left me for a Rockstar. Fuck him. Fuck her. "But one small breakup shouldn't have to be the end of something that was otherwise great for you. Please, for me, try North Carolina just one more time. And this time, I'm ready to go with you."

Why did she have to be such an optimist all of a sudden? Where was my normal pessimistic friend? One shopping trip to the mall outside of business hours and she was ready to change her whole world. Or maybe this push wasn't for her benefit, but for mine. Maybe she thought I was better in North Carolina, and this was her doing whatever she could to try to help me get better. I really don't think the location made much of a difference for me. I'd really cared for Emma. But I'd lied about my panic attacks. They'd never lessened when we dated. Actually, they were probably worse each night while I was with her.

"Okay. Let's do it. Let's move to North Carolina. Let's be roommates. Let's get my old job back. Let's try this."

"Really?"

"Yes, really."

I said it for her benefit, not my own. Because the day that library finished its renovations, she might move back into the safety of her dome and never leave again. As her friend, I had to try to help her take this giant leap. It might be the only time she ever tried. I would do anything for her. Including move back to the town where my ex-girlfriend and her Rockstar boyfriend lived.

~ CHAPTER 12 ~

AMANDA

"This is beautiful," Ellie said—my current customer. She had her sleeve rolled up, and in the mirror at my station she admired the new ink on her arm.

This tattoo made number twenty-three. I couldn't believe it. Twenty-three tattoos in my signature sketch design! Each better than the last, I thought, except for maybe the first, the original that started it all, which was somewhere, who knows where, in the world.

"Thanks, girl," Ellie said, giving me a hug. She was a regular, one of the shop's best customers. The type of person who didn't have many spots left for ink. "I love it. I'll bandage it up on my own. At this point, I know what I'm doing." She gave me a wink, then left me, heading down the hall for the breakroom. Ellie was so regular, she practically lived here. She and John were close friends.

"No," said a voice. A voice that was almost familiar to me. A voice that made me stop still. "No, it's gray. Old looking. Well worn. It's been about two months since I was here."

"I don't know, man," Patrick, the new guy, responded. I could hear his loud voice from my station. "I haven't seen it. If it's not in the box, I don't know what to tell you. We don't keep things forever. Eventually we donate them."

"Well, is Amanda here? I'd like to speak with her about it. She did my tattoo that night."

Fuck. I nearly tripped over my own feet. I realized right then and there it was *him. Oh God, it was him!*

"She's with a customer," Patrick said.

"Yeah, she's with a customer," another voice echoed. Finn's voice. Not his regular voice either. He used his 'guard-dog, I-will-break-you-in-half' voice. He must have noticed Nick or something and gone over thinking he was 'handling' the situation. "Why don't you write your name and phone number down on a piece of paper? We'll give you a call if it turns up. If Amanda remembers what happened to it. But I think it's unlikely she'd remember you from two months ago."

I swallowed, feeling jittery. Nick's hat was here, right inside the top drawer of my desk, right where it had been since that night he got me pregnant. I'd spent the last three weeks vomiting my guts out because of this guy. I thought for sure I would never see him again. At least not anytime soon. At least not without me having to track him down. Now he was back? Was his hat the only reason he was back? Would he have just picked it up and left already had it been in the lost-and-found box?

I worked up some kind of courage, grabbed the hat from my drawer, and left my station. I went to the front. Finn stared at me with bug eyes as I approached, as if to say, *'this guy you screwed, he's back, what should we do?'*

I ignored Finn. My eyes were on Nick's. It was impossibly hard facing him again. I'd been through every emotion in the book these last few weeks. I couldn't go a single day without thinking of him, thanks to the little life now living inside me. And the worst part was, I bet he'd barely thought of me at all. He'd probably thought more about this hat than of me. "It's here," I said. I reached across the counter, Finn directly to my right now, and I handed Nick his hat.

He took it. He even slipped it on. It was May now, and probably almost eighty degrees outside, but he put it on anyway. He smiled at me. "Thanks for holding on to it for me. I appreciate that."

I melted. I couldn't help it. Like a slab of butter on the hot pavement, a few words out of his mouth, and I was done for. He was more handsome than I remembered. His smile more perfect. His eyes a richer color. The hat looked pretty damn good on him. He had to know that. He came back because he knew this particular hat looked *that* good on him.

I noticed a woman. For a second, I wasn't entirely sure whether she'd come in with Nick or not. She hung by the door, in a black sweatshirt with the hood up and sunglasses covering most of her face. From what I could see, she was gorgeous. I decided she must be with Nick. Why wouldn't she be? Why wouldn't he have some gorgeous girlfriend already? It had been two months since our night together, plenty of time for him to meet and fall in love with some beautiful woman such as this one. The way she had her hood up like that—acting like she was too good for this place and didn't want to get too close to touch anything. I figured, yeah, she belonged with Nick.

It stung though. It really fucking stung. Finn must have come to the same conclusion as me about the woman by the door. Because he draped an arm over my shoulder, pulling me in against his side, putting on a show like I was his girl or something. "You need anything else, turtle guy?"

"Nick," the woman whispered. She had the softest, smallest voice. But one word out of her mouth and Nick responded.

"I don't need anything else. Not today. Goodbye, Amanda." He stepped backward for the door, moving in her direction.

A second later, he was holding open the door for the woman in the hoodie. She went past him carefully. Then the two of them disappeared. The moment the door closed, I curled into Finn's chest. "That was the worst," I whispered, trying to fight off the tears that wanted to come flooding.

"I know," Finn muttered. "Nick's an asshole. He's an asshole for bringing the girl in here like that. Right in front of you. Showing her off."

I don't know if he'd been showing her off, she was in a hoodie and wore sunglasses, but I knew what Finn meant. At the very least, Nick could have asked his girlfriend to wait in the car.

"I am so lost," Patrick commented, running his hands through his long, wild, untamed curls. "Can someone fill me in?"

Great. Now I had to tell another person my life problems. Thanks, Nick.

~ CHAPTER 13 ~

NICK

Blood passing through my ears—this thump, thump, thump—was always the first symptom. A small sound that grew so loud, it drowned out everything else. A panic attack for me always came on suddenly, without warning, sometimes when I was doing nothing more than taking a shower or lying in my bed at night. Actually, I never minded when a panic attack hit me in those places. I preferred it. In those places, at those times, no one had to know or see. But this one started just after leaving *Kill Devil Ink*, just after sitting down and starting my car in the parking lot.

It was a beautiful sunny day. Lou, in the passenger seat beside me, gushed over her accomplishment. We'd been back in town almost two weeks now, and this was the first time I'd taken her around other people since our twelve-hour drive from Maine. "I did it. I went inside with you. Did you see all the tattoos on that big guy?! I've never seen anything like him. He was like a man straight out of a romance novel!"

My hands on the steering wheel were tingling, like pins and needles. My vision turned dark and spotted with stars. Suddenly, I was hot and sweaty. So hot I wanted to strip off my shirt. I didn't, though, because I knew what was happening. "Two minutes, Lou," I breathed, my voice caught in my throat. "Give me… two minutes."

I hopped out of the car. *You're dying.* I wasn't dying. I knew better. *You're fucking dying. Say goodbye now. You'll die on this pavement, get run over like a pancake, and the pretty tattoo artist girl will find your dead, squished corpse.*

I sank to the pavement, my head between my knees, and tried to breathe.

Shit. *Why here? Why now?* I'd been okay a second ago. Now I felt like I was about to black out. It could have been two minutes. It could have been ten. It could have been an hour. Time was impossible to measure. But eventually the intensity on my chest lifted. My full sight returned. I gained enough strength in my muscles, and I was able to stand. I pushed against the tire of my car, making black marks on my hands, and I stood to my feet.

"Is everything okay?"

Oh God. It wasn't Lou. She was in the car where I had left her. She knew all I wanted when I had a panic attack was to be left alone. The voice was Amanda's. She must have followed me outside. In my head the attack had lasted forever; in reality I bet only two minutes or so had been spent in my own personal hell on the pavement.

"You okay?" she asked again.

"Yes." Other than the extreme exhaustion I now felt, I was fine.

"Okay. I thought you'd tripped or something." She'd hadn't seen me trip. She'd seen everything that had just happened. I was willing to bet money on it, judging by the concern on her face.

"I'm fine. Just a small stomachache. Did you need something?" I asked. Dammit, under different circumstances, I would have liked to have had a conversation with her. We certainly had plenty of unfinished business we could have been getting to. That night we'd spent together, getting each other off as many times as humanly possible, had been pretty damn incredible. If she was into it, I'd be up for another round. But up for talking about what just happened—nope, not ever.

"No, I didn't need anything," she said, stepping back. "Just saying goodbye. Goodbye, Nick."

She remembered my name. I liked that she knew it, and for whatever reason, I liked that she'd followed me outside. She started to turn away, but I called after her.

"Hey."

She paused.

"You and your guy sure looked cozy again. Seems like that relationship is going well for you." I referred to Meat Head inside. I'd noticed the way he made a show of putting his arm around her in front of me.

"Finn and I never stopped being cozy. Our relationship is great."

She was such a liar. "You're so full of shit," I muttered, calling her out. I moved a little closer to her. She wasn't with him. Maybe she had him wrapped around her finger, but she wasn't with him. I just knew she wasn't. She wouldn't be out here talking to me if she was. I felt my guard slipping, and quickly. "My tattoo isn't finished. I think there's more to it than the turtle and the ship. What do you think?"

She stared at me.

I stepped closer.

I couldn't help myself. Maybe I still felt jittery and vulnerable, a little out of control from my panic attack, maybe that's what was pushing me to do this, but I moved my hands to her neck and my lips to hers. I kissed her. I touched her face. I breathed in her air. I pressed close to her body.

She kissed me back—hard. Hard enough that I knew with even more certainty that Meat Head Finn guy wasn't with her.

She didn't fight me. She didn't try to act like she didn't want it either. She simply let go right along with me. It was the nicest thing I'd felt in weeks. A feeling so polar opposite to the one I'd just experienced on the pavement.

I broke away first.

"Sorry," I muttered. "I got black stuff on your face." It had been on my hands from when I'd touched my car's tire trying to stand.

She was damn adorable. She had her pale pink hair pulled back in a ponytail, all these small pieces falling loose around her face. She wore a white t-shirt, tight over her tits. And I loved the way she looked at me. Like I fucking ruled the world. Too bad Emma never once looked at me like that. Thinking about Emma pissed me off. Thinking about the effect she still had on my life bothered me. I wanted to see Amanda again, I decided. I wanted inside her again. Because she'd been a pretty great distraction the night we'd been together. If I had to be back here in North Carolina, I was going to need a distraction like her.

"I'll call the shop and set up an appointment with you for more work on my tattoo," I told her, moving closer to my car. "You good with that?"

"That works."

Fuck, I couldn't just get in my car and go. I stepped back to her for one more kiss. I took it from her, getting just one more taste, before I got back in the car.

I watched her for a second as she stepped away and hurried back inside *Kill Devil Ink*.

"Wow," Lou whispered. "That was weird watching you kiss her. You and Misty Preston used to make out in the library sometimes, so I've seen you kiss girls before. But that was weirdly innocent on your part."

"You used to spy on me and Misty Preston?!" My mouth dropped open.

"Hey, don't feel too special, I spied on everyone in the library. I didn't give you special preference."

That was a little creepy. Coming from someone else I would have been weirded out. But Lou was too much of a sweetheart to weird anyone out. "What do you mean *'weirdly innocent?'"*

"You were gentler with her. I don't know. Careful with her. You savored her kiss. With Misty you used to kiss her like you were in a race or something."

Misty was a girlfriend I barely even liked. I went out with her, like most of the girls I dated in high school, because that was what everyone did at my high school. They dated. They made out in libraries between study sessions. They touched each other under the table, between bookshelves, in the backseat of their cars. I hope Lou didn't see me do everything I'd done back then.

"I like Amanda," I explained to Lou. "That's the difference you just saw."

"Oh. Okay. I get it."

She didn't get it at all. Lou had only ever viewed the world through a looking glass. Last night, I had to teach her how to use the TV remote. She'd read every book under the sun, but Netflix was a whole new concept for her. "Alright. Let's go home now. I think that's enough excitement for one day."

~ CHAPTER 14 ~

AMANDA

I touched my fingers to my lips.

He kissed me. I couldn't believe he kissed me again.

So easily too. About two milliseconds after he left, I decided I needed to stop him and tell him that I was pregnant, in case I never got another chance. I would just blurt it out—get the words out into the world. He deserved to know I was having his kid. It was the right thing to do. The honest thing to do. Whatever he thought of me, even if the news made him cringe or scream or hug me—I just had to do it. I had to say the words.

And then, I hadn't said anything at all.

When I saw him, he was crouched on the pavement in the shade of his car. The parking lot was calm and quiet. The woman in the hoodie was already inside the car. Nick had his head between his legs. His breathing was rapid and his hands, squeezing the fabric of his knit hat, were trembling. I initially thought he was about to vomit on the pavement. I couldn't decide if I should go up to him or turn around and go back inside, giving him his privacy.

I couldn't walk away, though. My feet were stuck. I watched him for a moment. This wasn't a person throwing up. This was something else, possibly a panic attack. I wasn't sure since I'd never had a panic attack myself nor seen anyone having one, other than on television.

He calmed quickly. It took only a minute or so before he stood up. He saw me. We had a conversation during which he pretended that whatever had just happened to him hadn't happened at all. I wondered for a moment if I'd imagined the whole thing, reading into things too much.

Then suddenly, after a few words about Finn, he kissed me. I felt so much in that kiss. I felt this fear in my chest for him, concern over whatever I'd just witnessed happening to him. I also felt his pain. I don't how or why, or what had just happened to him, but whatever it was it came through in the way he kissed me. All calm and slow and careful. Almost like a cry for someone to help ease that pain. It wasn't like all the kisses we'd shared that first night. Those kisses were pure lust and desire. This wasn't the same.

I didn't tell him about the baby. The timing didn't feel right. He said he wanted to add to his tattoo. Maybe he really wanted more ink. Or maybe he wanted an excuse to see me again. Either way, I walked away on a high. I couldn't stop smiling.

"What happened?" Finn wanted to know the very second I walked back in through the door. Patrick stared at me too, standing shoulder-to-shoulder with Finn.

"Nothing."

"Why are you smiling?"

"I'm not."

I was and I couldn't stop.

That giddy feeling stuck with me the rest of the day. Made me feel hopeful.

It faded by Thursday, though, when no one named Nick had called the shop to set up an appointment. By the weekend, I felt stupid all over again. What was with this guy and his control over me? I didn't like it. I didn't like waiting all week on him.

It was Sunday night. Someone named Lou had an appointment booked with me late in the day. Apparently, another person wanting one of my sketch designs. I was waiting for this appointment, when Nick stepped into my station.

I caught my breath.

He meandered in like we knew each other well, and he sat in the extra chair I had beside my desk. It wasn't a great day for me today. I'd thrown up three times already. Just looking at food was making me queasy. I was more exhausted than ever. But having him so close, having him almost sit at my desk with me, was like a shot of adrenaline.

He unfolded a piece of computer paper and flattened it on my desk. It was a picture of his tattoo, the one straight off his butt. "I thought this might help you. As far as drawing on it and adding to the tattoo I already have. I don't have any ideas. I thought you might know what's supposed to go next."

"Did you xerox your butt?" I joked.

He smiled—a smile that touched his eyes. "You're funny." His eyes connected with mine, and his attention did crazy things to my chest.

"I have an appointment with someone named Lou," I whispered. "You can't be here now."

"I'm Lou. I mean, my friend is Lou. She made the appointment. I let her call for me. Although, she was supposed to make the appointment in my name, not her own. Sorry about that. So you didn't know I was coming?"

"No."

"I'm sorry. I didn't mean for that to happen."

He hadn't? I touched his piece of paper. "This is 2D, your ass is 3D."

"I'm sorry?"

"I mean, can I just draw straight on your skin instead?"

He sat back in his chair. "Oh, sure."

"I'm not too experienced with free-styling on skin though. Maybe I should get John and get his opinion."

"I don't want John's opinion. Fuck his opinion. I didn't come in here for his design on my skin. I came in here for yours."

He moved to stand up, apprehension be damned, and he unbuttoned his pants before plopping himself, stomach first, onto my chair. He inched his pants down just enough so I could see his left butt cheek. His previous ink was right there where I'd put it. He had a nice ass. If I turned his current design into one that fully covered his whole left cheek...

Fuck, it would look nice.

Not that his ass didn't already look nice. But yeah, I pictured the possibility. And it was sexy as hell.

"I have this idea."

"Go for it. I didn't know how much I'd love the sails on the turtle until you put them there. I know whatever's in your head is going to be awesome."

He did? How did he know that?

I didn't have that same confidence in myself. I took an alcohol wipe and began using it to sterilize his skin. I had my red pen out, the one for temporary drawing, and began sketching. All these ideas quickly started swirling in my head. I let them take over. It wasn't about *'what should I do,'* it became *'what shouldn't I do.'* I drew an ocean around his turtle in the form of lines and angles. A horizon, the sun as a compass pointing north. I had clouds and sky and the legs of an octopus reaching out of the water for his turtle.

Nick's eyes were on me while I drew my design. "Is that your dad?" he asked at one point. He meant the picture on my desk, the only picture I had on my desk, the one of me and Dad at the Nags Head Fishing Pier. *His favorite place. And my favorite person.*

"Yes."

"Is he a fisherman?"

"Not in the sense that he had a boat and that it was his career. He just liked to fish off that pier almost every day of the year. Couldn't keep him from it." I don't know if it was my pregnancy hormones taking over or what but speaking about Dad with Nick got to me. Dad would never get to meet my baby. Tears burned behind my eyes. I bit down on the inside of my cheek, fighting them off so he wouldn't notice how hard his question hit.

"He's gone," Nick discerned. "I'm sorry you lost him."

"It's just me now."

"Your mom?"

"She left a long time ago." I swallowed hard. Speaking about my parents didn't normally choke me up. *Why was it affecting me so easily talking about it with Nick?*

He moved his arm and rested his hand on my knee. He squeezed gently. It was really, truly kind of him.

"Your parents?" I asked him now. I wanted to put some heat on him in return, see how he handled the same question.

"Both alive. Both around. They live in Maine. My mom's especially overbearing. I'm surprised she hasn't tried calling me three times since I've been lying here."

I smiled. He sounded fond of her, of both of them. "Okay," I said. I'd finished my sketch on his skin with the temporary pen. "It's... um... big." I bit down on my lip. "I don't know if this is what you had in mind at all." I peeled off my gloves, tossing them in the trash, and grabbed my phone for a picture.

He pushed up on his elbows, twisting his body in an attempt to see what I'd done. "I like it, you can start." He laid back down.

"Want to see it from my angle first?"

"No. I've seen all your other designs you have posted online. I don't think you could fuck this up even if you tried."

"You looked me up?" He had my heart trying to beat itself right out of my chest.

"Yes." He touched my leg again. And that smile I loved so much of his came out on his lips. I decided that he was, hands down, my most favorite customer I'd ever had. "Okay, let's get started then."

~ CHAPTER 15 ~

NICK

Not gonna lie, I didn't give a damn about what Amanda was adding to my tattoo. I trusted her enough. I know I should have worried a little more, since this would be on my skin for life, but I hadn't come in today for the tattoo. It was her I came in for. The tattoo was only an excuse.

She worked differently this time. Less on guard, more at ease. She was talented, and I don't think she knew that about herself the first time we'd met. I'd been truthful with her. I'd been following her online, checking out the different photos she'd been posting of the ink she'd been doing over the last two months. I wanted to believe my little turtle had sparked something in her. Because she also had pictures posted of her work prior to my turtle. They were good and all, but nothing compared to her more recent work.

I figured, one butt cheek... a small sacrifice on my part in an effort to help her continue to grow. Because the Nick from six months ago would never have wanted something this large on his skin. But I wanted this. I couldn't wait to see what this woman would dream up without limits.

I also wanted to ask her out to dinner.

As she began with the tattoo gun, putting real ink into my skin, it was all I could think about. She had my heart pounding right out of my chest. The words were there on the tip of my tongue, wanting out, but I had a hard time saying them. Crazy because even Emma hadn't been this difficult to ask out the first time around. The thing was... if Amanda said no, it would make this appointment awkward as hell. If she said no, that would be that, no second chances, because I couldn't keep coming in here asking for more and more tattoos from the girl who'd turned me down.

"Can you pull your pants down a little more? I need to..." She fumbled on her words, her cheeks turning pink. "I need you to uncover your whole butt. Your other cheek, I mean, so I can get a little closer to the... the edge."

"Closer to my crack?" I smiled.

"Exactly."

The blush on her cheeks was the most adorable thing in the world. I wondered where, on other guy's bodies, she'd put tattoos before. Was it only my ass that made her blush like this? Or all of them? Because if it was me making her blush, maybe asking her out would be easier than I feared.

I inched down my pants.

"Wait." She set down her tattoo gun and hopped out of her chair. She grabbed a towel from a shelf on the wall and brought it to me. I took it. Then, crossing her arms over her chest, she turned around. I guess she meant for me to cover my front with the towel because there really was no way around pulling my pants down without freeing my junk.

"Fuck," she whispered.

I stared at her back, at the way her pretty pink ponytail fell, at the skin exposed on her neck. I wanted to put my hands on her, to feel her skin, and it did not help that my cock, as I let my jeans fall, was now in open air, with only a towel to keep it in line.

I carefully lay back down on the chair on my stomach. "Okay, Amanda," I muttered, swallowing.

She turned back around, her eyes meeting mine. She wheeled her chair closer, close enough that I could feel her warmth. She leaned over me, her tits almost close enough to graze against my side, as she started tattooing me once more.

I shut my eyes, growling in my frustration, because she had me hard as fuck. Hard enough to pound nails. It was uncomfortable lying there, thinking how much I wanted to be inside her, right here in her chair, right this very second.

"Nick? Hi."

Fuck. Me. Sideways.

I picked my head up. Because someone else had said my name. And I recognized the voice. Sure enough, I opened my eyes to Emma Winchester.

Kill. Me. Now.

That helped me get rid of my erection. Someone might as well have dumped ice water over my body. Emma stood with her Rockstar boyfriend, Caleb Mills, in the entryway to Amanda's tiny station. He was *literally* a famous Rockstar. And I had my pants at my fucking ankles with my ass on display for the both of them. Not exactly an ideal way to run into your ex.

"Hi, Emma," I said, trying to be polite.

"I thought you'd moved back to Maine a couple months ago."

"No. Nope, I'm still in town."

"Oh."

She seemed disappointed. Amanda stopped working and stood. She bumped into her desk and something clattered to the ground. She didn't bend over to pick it up. "Would you excuse me, Nick? I need to use the bathroom."

She walked away, past Emma and Caleb, in a hurry. She muttered a 'hello' and a 'great to see you' as she passed, leading me to believe they knew each other well. But I'd already figured that much. Everybody knew everybody around here.

Emma made more polite small talk. She asked about my job. "Save any animals today?"

"Not today."

"How's it been going otherwise?"

"Fine," I assured her, not wanting to say anything more on the subject.

"Well, it was good seeing you, Nick. Take care," Emma said, finally ending the conversation, finally leaving me alone.

Well, that made me feel like shit. She'd completely moved on. While I was getting a tattoo the size of China on my ass rather than being man enough to just ask this woman out.

I lay there for almost ten more minutes before Amanda returned. She looked flushed, sweaty even. Her breathing was heavier. I even noticed her hands were shaking.

"What's wrong?" I asked her.

"I'm tired. I haven't been sleeping lately. Can we stop here? I'll take lots of pictures to mark where I'm at in the design, and then you can schedule another appointment for another day. This tattoo will actually take a few more sessions to finish. Does that work for you?"

Her big brown eyes—I swear they were close to tears.

"Yes," I said. Whatever she needed.

I couldn't figure out what had happened, what I'd said wrong; if it was

Emma, if it was my ass, or if it was something else entirely. Had something happened in the bathroom? Had someone hurt her? Finn... where was that asshole today? Was it something to do with him?

"You okay?" I asked again.

"I'm fine. Just tired, like I already said."

She definitely wasn't fine. I wished I knew how I could help her. But she was being stubborn as hell. I let her take her pictures and bandage my ass, then I pulled up my pants. But I didn't plan on leaving until she gave me some reassurance that she was okay.

~ CHAPTER 16 ~

AMANDA

Oh gosh. I'd barely eaten today. And yet, once again, the nauseated feeling struck me. Right when Emma showed up too. My stomach just rolled over on itself. I could see how awkward this was for Nick. His whole body went tense. I wanted to stay. I wanted to say something that might make this less awkward for him. But throwing up all over the floor would have been more mortifying for everyone.

I excused myself and hurried away.

In the bathroom, I kneeled on the floor by the toilet, waiting for the inevitable, but nothing happened. Little beads of sweat formed on my forehead, while I willed myself to *just get it over with.* It wasn't exactly well ventilated in the shop's small bathroom, and I felt miserable. After a few minutes, I gave up. But I hung around longer, trying to cool down.

Eventually, I went back to Nick. Back to where I'd left him. Emma was gone. *Thank God.* Frankly, there wasn't a chance in hell I could continue working feeling as shaky as I now felt. Since I'd found out I was pregnant, I'd been determined not to let it slow me down. But I couldn't continue today. I said everything I could to end our appointment, and he agreed to come back another day, another time.

We were checking out at the register. Nick had his credit card out to pay. Patrick was working tonight, helping two attractive women, both in their mid-twenties, close to my age. One was trying to decide which sea turtle she wanted on her ankle. I gave Nick a look because she was pointing to a picture on the wall where he'd found his design. *She was about to pick the same turtle he originally chose the night we met!* The turtle I talked him out of getting.

"It's her," I whispered, initially excited.

He shook his head, fighting a smile.

"Nick, she could be your turtle soulmate," I muttered under my breath, completely teasing him. I grabbed his hand across the counter, I couldn't help myself.

"Stop." He grinned. "She isn't."

"You sure?"

"I'm sure."

"I love this turtle," we heard the woman say to her friend. My eyes widened at her words. "But what kind of butterflies do you have? I've always wanted a butterfly in this spot."

"Shucks," I whispered, my eyes still locked on Nick's. "Maybe next time you'll find her." I'd been joking around, but I also found myself relieved the woman hadn't decided on his same turtle. And it wasn't even his turtle, not the one he had on his skin anyway, but I still didn't want her to have it. Maybe I'd take that picture off the wall later tonight.

Nick moved his hand, lacing his fingers with mine. "That's not my girl. It's got to be on her ass, remember?" *I had mentioned something about his 'turtle-ass-soulmate,' hadn't I?* "You looking for any new ink?"

Wait. "What?" I whispered. Was he suggesting I get the turtle on my ass?

He smiled. "What are you doing right now?" he said instead, changing the subject.

"Me?"

Right this moment I was having trouble focusing on anything beyond the fact that we were holding hands over the top of the counter. The same counter I looked at every day of my life. The same counter I'd stood at with countless customers before him. The same counter, actually, he'd had me on top of, naked, my legs spread open wide, his mouth...

"Yes, you," he confirmed, becoming playful with me now. "Because I really don't want to leave this business again without asking you out. Not a mistake I'd like to keep making."

I froze.

I hadn't seen that coming.

My heart, already racing under my shirt, pounded harder, pounded so hard I was feeling almost weak.

"If you're too tired, I get it, maybe another day. But I'd love if you came over and had dinner at my place tonight."

I opened my mouth to speak, quick to give him some sort of excuse, but then I closed it as fast as I'd opened it. I'd been on my feet or hunched over doing ink all day. My back ached. My stomach was still queasy. I wanted a shower, or possibly a bath, and to crawl into bed for the rest of the week. But I didn't want to say no. I didn't want him to walk away again either. So my answer was easy.

"Yes," I agreed.

He bit down on his lip. "Good." Then he took a breath. "I live with a roommate. Lou. She'll be home. It's likely we won't see her, though. She mostly keeps to her space in the house.

Lou—the same person who made his appointment today. Was she also the girl in the hoodie?

"When is your last appointment?"

"You were my last appointment."

"Great."

"I need to clean up my station." I breathed out. "I need to set up for tomorrow." I needed to go home, shower, change clothes, redo my hair and makeup. I needed someone to splash some cold water in my face. I needed him to stop staring at me like that. Like he wanted to fuck me on this counter all over again. Because it was impossibly hot in this room. And I needed to know how to be a normal human being around this guy. Because normal was the furthest thing from what I felt.

"I'll help you do all that." He moved his hand away from mine.

"Really?"

"Of course."

Nick was super obliging. He listened and did whatever I asked as far as helping me clean up and prep for tomorrow. What did all of this mean? Dinner? His place? Staying to help me after work? I could feel my excitement growing. Our first night together had been purely physical. Was this the same? Or was it more?

~ CHAPTER 17 ~

NICK

I had Amanda in my car. This beautiful pink-haired, tattooed, sexy—*so fucking sexy*—woman. She had these bubbly flower tattoos all down her left arm. Pinks and greens, teals and purples. I spotted strawberries mixed in there. I don't know why I never noticed the strawberries before, but I could see them now. Little heart-shaped strawberries. She was about one thousand times cooler than me. I was the kid who couldn't fit in with anyone, even my family. My only true friend growing up was a homeless girl in a library. But Amanda—one look at her and I could just tell, she knew exactly what the fuck she was doing with her life. She had this job and this life as this tattoo artist. I could picture it, and it made me wonder why the hell she'd just agreed to have dinner with me.

I could tell she was exhausted. Today had been a long day for her. I had this urge to take her home. Take her to bed with me. Hold her in my arms. Take her clothes off too, if I was being completely honest with myself. Keep her all to myself. That was the introvert in me—this need to revert to my safe place. But it surprised me, that I had the urge to pull her into that space with me.

Still, if all that happened between us tonight was dinner, I'd be happy with that. Really, I just wanted to find out *why* she made me have all these urges in the first place.

She freed her hair from her hair-tie, shaking out her strands of pink, combing her fingers through the pieces. I could smell her—lavender. Fuck me. I was trying to play it as cool as possible. Because I wasn't cool, not in the least. And she was making it so difficult.

I turned the radio on; music while I drove calmed my nerves. But when I recognized a *Sunset Revival* song, I immediately turned it off again. Emma's new Rockstar boyfriend was part of the band *Sunset Revival*, the lead singer actually, and I couldn't bear to hear their music or his voice. Shame, because I used to be a fan.

"It must be awkward running into her and him all the time in this small town," Amanda commented, looking out her window. I guess she'd also recognized the song on the radio. Clearly, I'd been about as transparent as possible.

"It was why I tried to move back home," I admitted.

"But you didn't?"

"I didn't."

She ran her hands over her jeans. Was I making her uncomfortable? I pulled down the street I lived on and turned into the driveway of my brand new rental. It was tucked back in the neighborhoods of Kill Devil Hills, not in the prime beachfront areas, not even walkable to the beach, but the street was quiet and I liked quiet.

"I'm going to go inside and talk to Lou," I told her, cutting off the ignition. "Lou is sensitive to a lot of things. I should warn her first that I'm bringing you inside. I'll just be a minute."

Amanda had to be wondering what the hell that meant. But she didn't complain, she simply nodded. So I jumped out of the car and rushed up the deck stairs that lead straight to the second level. "Lou," I yelled once I got inside.

I found Lou on the couch, right next to me.

"Jesus Christ, don't do that," she whispered as she stood up. She held the book she'd been reading over her chest like it was a shield. "You can't just run in here like a crazy person. You almost gave me a heart attack."

"I'm sorry." I was out of breath. I knew better than that. I knew better than to startle Lou. She'd been making so much progress navigating new things lately. I didn't want to make a wrong move and hinder that in any way. "I have Amanda with me. She's in my car outside. I offered to make her dinner here. What do you think?"

In a split second, I could see the panic in Lou's eyes. I immediately realized I probably shouldn't have sprung this on her so suddenly.

"She's really calm," I said to Lou, in an attempt to fix the damage I'd already created. "She's been gentle when she does ink on me. She doesn't say much while she's working, but when she does, she has this soft, sweet voice. She's not full of shit either. She talked me out of the original turtle tattoo I wanted, that I admit now was totally lame. She's patient, and a little OCD. Which I can tell by the way she keeps her workstation so impossibly clean at *Kill Devil Ink*. I really like this girl. You will, too. I would have taken her out to a restaurant, but I know somehow that isn't her style either. Trust me, Lou. She's safe. She's safe like us. I know she is."

Lou was scared of just about everyone. Which was why I still couldn't believe she'd walked into *Kill Devil Ink* so bravely last week. Then again, it had been for just a small moment and she hadn't been anywhere since.

"She gave you a panic attack."

"It wasn't her." We'd been over this already. About a million times actually. "Mine aren't triggered by anything. They just happen."

"Whatever. I'm going to my room."

"You should have dinner with us. Help me figure this girl out. You're better at reading people than I am." I took a step back toward the door. I could see now Lou had relaxed some. She was going to be okay. She wasn't completely happy with me, but she'd be okay. Also, I felt bad for making Amanda wait so long in the car.

I'd been living with Lou for over a week now. It was already exhausting sometimes—taking care of her, walking on eggshells for her. I didn't know how much I could push her out of her comfort zone, or if she was even comfortable here at all. Maybe bringing her here was not the right move. But Amanda. I could not miss this opportunity. Every cell in my body was screaming at me—*don't fuck this up.*

I hurried back outside.

Down the wooden stairs.

Back to my car in the driveway.

I opened her door.

"Hey," I said, all out of breath.

"Nick." She didn't move out of my car. She sat there, her blue eyes staring up at me, pleading with me somehow. "I don't know if I should be here."

I took a deep, calming breath. It was dark out now, the air thick and black. I could hear crickets chirping. "Why not?" I know we both felt something here. Why not see what it was?

"You're a client. A million other reasons. I barely know you. I don't know what the situation is with your roommate. Or what she means to you.

If you're even over Emma. If you even like me. It's all confusing. I really don't like being this confused."

"Lou has agoraphobia." I just blurted it out, when it wasn't my truth to tell. Somehow I needed Amanda to know and to trust me. "She's my friend from back home. My best friend, actually. I'm trying to protect her and push her out of her comfort zone at the same time. She's just a friend. More like my little sister. I'm not over Emma. Not really. Not fully. She fucked me up pretty good earlier this year. Seeing her today did not sit well in my stomach. But every moment I'm with you feels good. Really good, actually. It's easy being around you. The night we spent together was kind of like breathing fresh air. Fuck, maybe just breathing for the first time. I want more of that feeling. I want to feel okay for once in my life. This is just dinner. Just my house. Well, my rental house. I'm not..."

I stopped talking because Amanda had tears in her eyes. Did I put them there? Shit, did I say way too much?

She stood up, making me have to take a step back to move out of her way. She pushed the passenger side door closed. "I want dinner."

She did? "You do."

"Yes."

"Well, okay. I'm not really much of a cook—but okay."

"Me neither. So anything you make will be an improvement from a normal night for me."

I smiled. I couldn't help it. She was amazing. Something about her. So fucking amazing.

~ CHAPTER 18 ~

AMANDA

Nick was quiet as he made some kind of pasta for the two of us. I sat at the table, waiting on him, taking in his rental house. It was fully furnished, and about five times bigger than my home.

I held a glass of wine in my hand, feeling a little like a fraud. He'd poured it for me, and I was pretending to sip it. Even not pregnant, I never was one to hold a wine glass in my hand. Mostly though, I'd never sat at a table while a man cooked for me—just waiting on him, while he waited on me.

Nick finished and he set the pasta plate in front of me. On any other day, this whole meal would have been amazing. But my stomach didn't want the pasta. And honestly, I shouldn't even have been pretending with the wine in my hand.

Nick took the seat across from me. I really got to study him, sitting face-to-face like we were, under the lighting of his dining room. He was handsome, *so fucking handsome,* why did he have to be so handsome? The line of his jaw, it was sharp as a razorblade. The dark stubble on his face that I knew was rough to the touch, I couldn't have tattooed it on any better. The Cupid's bow at the top of his lips, had to make other women blush like it did me. Mostly, the way the blue in his eyes contrasted with his dark lashes, made my stomach swirl each time we made eye contact. Not to mention that smirk on his face. That smirk that was always there. His beautiful half-smirk was going to kill me, going to be the fucking end of me, because I couldn't breathe when he looked at me straight on like he was doing right this minute. This man was too handsome. It didn't make any sense that I had his undivided attention right this minute. There was just too much perfection happening in front of me.

"I'm pregnant."

I just blurted it out.

Fuck.

I don't know what made me say it, maybe his pretty blue eyes, but the words just leaped straight out of my mouth. But even worse... was the word vomit that came next.

"It's Finn's baby. It just sort of happened. Before we happened. And yeah. So, yeah. I'm pregnant. Super pregnant. I thought you should know that."

Well, that got rid of the smirk on his face. It died in a second. But as calm as ever, Nick reached across the space and took the wine glass from my hand. "If you're pregnant, you shouldn't be drinking that." He took it from me and he brought it to his own lips. He drank down the liquid in only a few quick gulps.

"I know," I whispered.

He finished my wine and set the empty glass down. "So you slept with Finn. Then you slept with me. You sure it isn't mine and not his?" He wasn't angry in the least as he asked this, just inquisitive.

"I'm sure."

Why was I lying?

Why was I so afraid to tell him it was his?

"How do you know for sure?"

"Well, I'm three months pregnant. Finn and I were sleeping together pretty regularly around three months ago. I was only with you two months ago. So, simple math." I bit down on my lip. Why the fuck was I so afraid to admit the truth to him? I wasn't three months pregnant—only two. It was his. And I'd never once been with Finn like that.

"Okay." He grabbed his own glass of wine and, in another couple gulps, finished that one as well. Then he sat back in his chair, pushing his pasta away, staring directly at me. "Where does that leave you and me? Are you dating Finn? Are you with Finn?"

"No. And no."

A ripple moved over his jaw. He breathed out through his nose.

I moved my hands to my lap. They were trembling so hard—I didn't want him to see.

He breathed out heavily again.

Should I ask him to take me home now? Was our night over? Did he hate me now?

"So I fucked you while you were already pregnant? With another man's kid?"

My chest tightened. "Yes." I swallowed. "Yes. I'm sorry. I didn't know."

"You don't need to apologize. I'm not criticizing you. I'm trying to straighten out the facts. Are you going to try with Finn? Try to be with him?"

"No. I don't want to be with him."

"And me? What do you want with me?"

It felt like I was strapped up to a lie detector test.

Nick left his chair. He stood up and went to the kitchen counter, he grabbed the bottle of wine, and brought it back to the table. He took a sip straight from the bottle this time as he stood close to my body. "Answer my question," he muttered, staring down at me from his tall height. "What do you want with me?"

"I like you," I whispered.

"How much do you like me?"

I could feel my face tingling. His direct scrutiny was about the most intense thing I'd ever felt. "Enough that I'm here now instead of anywhere else." Everything else might have been a lie, but that was the cold, hard truth.

He set the bottle down on the table. He leaned over me, moving closer to me. His hands went to my face. They were warm. They were gentle. "Do you have a plan with Finn?"

"I don't have any plans with him."

"Then let me be your plan."

My neck was aching from the angle I was staring up at him. I had no idea what his words meant. *Let me be your plan.* Like he wanted to step in and do this with me even though he believed Finn was the father? Was that what he meant?

"Come with me," he whispered.

One of his hands moved from my neck, over my shoulder, and to my arm. He tugged, wanting me to stand with him. I did. I was still working on wrapping my brain around those words. *Let me be your plan.* Still trying to make sense of them. If he really, truly meant them then they were the nicest words anyone had ever said to me. My chest was burning because of them. On fire and cracked wide open, exposed, and feeling more than I remember ever feeling before in my life.

I followed him away from the open living room and down the hall. I'd never been more terrified, more curious, or more exuberant, nevertheless all at once, in my whole life. This man—he might just be exactly what I'd always   needed.

~ CHAPTER 19 ~

NICK

I pulled Amanda into the bathroom. Pushing aside the shower curtain, I started the water. Lou was nosey, part of her nature was spying on others, and just in case she was listening right now, I felt I needed complete privacy with Amanda. The locked bathroom door and the sound of the shower, even the humidity from the water, gave me the comfort that I had the privacy I needed.

I moved my hands back to Amanda's neck. I pressed my forehead to hers. The way she stared up at me, like she needed me so completely, was dependent on each word that came out of my mouth, had me wanting to drop to my knees for this woman.

She had Finn's baby inside her. Maybe a better man would have pushed her to go to Finn, pushed her to try with him, but I wasn't that man. The only thing I felt when she'd told me the baby was his—was this fear of losing her. She wasn't even mine to lose. But whatever I had with her; I couldn't give it up. I'd spent only that one night with her. But I couldn't help the way I felt. Or the way I couldn't let her go.

Now... I wanted to kiss her so bad, I was vibrating with need. "Is it a boy or a girl?" I muttered.

"I don't know yet."

"Have you been going to the doctor?"

"I've had a couple appointments."

"Good." I swallowed.

I stared at her for a moment. The steam from the shower made everything grow warmer. I couldn't bring myself to turn it off. Hell, I couldn't even break eye contact with her.

She must have felt the same heat growing too because she whispered, "Why'd you turn on the shower?"

"I needed privacy with you."

I closed my eyes, taking a deep breath.

"Nick." She moved her hands to my face. She ran her fingers over the stubble I needed to shave. I wanted to kiss her, more than kiss her, but I resisted making that move because... was it wrong? Was it wrong to want to be inside her now when I knew she was pregnant with someone else's kid? Because I wanted her exactly the same way I'd had her that first night. The thickening humidity in the air wasn't helping. Anxiety bubbled under the surface of my skin, and the fear that a panic attack might overwhelm me right this moment was also there. But I ignored it because everything else was more important than any of my normal fears.

"I really like you, Nick," she muttered. She touched her lips to mine, carefully. I didn't move to kiss her back, not yet at least. "I haven't been able to stop thinking about you since that night we were together."

She was going to be my undoing. Words like that... mixed with how amazing her body felt close to mine. "Same," I muttered. Thoughts of her hadn't left my mind since that day, either.

Fuck it.

Why fight it?

Right?

I pressed my lips to hers, and I took the kiss I'd been so desperately craving. She felt good—so damn good. Her lips were soft, warm, and her mouth opened to mine. I tasted her tongue. I dug my fingers into her pretty pink hair. I couldn't hold on to even a shred of self-control. I lost it all the moment my tongue met hers.

She had her hands on my stomach. She pushed up the fabric of my shirt, working to get it off my body. My mouth only broke from hers for the small moment it took to remove my shirt over my head. I let it fall to the floor and then I made quick work of getting her undressed.

In seconds she was down to her bra and panties, while I was down to only my boxer briefs. I pulled back, biting down hard on my bottom lip, moving my hands to my hair.

"Let's slow down," I muttered. My heart was racing about a million miles an hour.

She nodded, looking almost ashamed.

I wasn't ashamed of anything. I just needed a moment to breathe, and to settle my spinning head. If I thought too much, I was afraid of the consequences that might follow. I wanted to believe my panic attacks came and went randomly, without much to do with anything at all. But maybe that wasn't entirely true. Maybe, when my head started spinning, maybe that had a little bit to do with their onset.

"Can we do this again tomorrow?" I asked. "Same time. I'll pick you up after work. I'll cook you dinner. I'll try harder to keep my clothes on."

"You want me to go now?"

Actually, no. But something about this entire conversation had my fingertips tingling, had my vision going a little spotty, had the blood pumping just a little too hard through my ears. "Do you want to stay?"

"Not if you want me to go."

"I don't want you to go. I need you to go. Tomorrow's better." I moved over to the shower, hitting the faucet to turn off the water. I took her hand in mine, not bothering to pick up my clothes. I know what I'd just said. But even I couldn't follow my own request. I led her out of the bathroom, down the hallway, hardly caring that we were walking around in our underwear. Lou's room was on the top level, so I knew she wouldn't see us.

"The lights stay off," I muttered. I tugged her into the dark of my room. I locked my door behind us. "Our clothes stay on," I added, for what little clothes we had left. I pulled her over to my bed. I knew I had only a few precious seconds left. I pushed down the covers and tugged her into bed with me. Then I curled into her body. I shut my eyes tight.

This wasn't sexual.

I might have wanted it to be, but my anxiety was about to get the better of me. She was about to see just how fucked up I really was. All the signs were there. The debilitating fear, the rush of adrenaline, the tightness in my chest, the pressure in my head. In three more seconds, I'd be having a panic attack. And Amanda was about to witness everything.

~ CHAPTER 20 ~

AMANDA

Nick rolled away from me, his muscular back to me like a wall in the dark. His breathing changed—it became heavier. At first his breathing was only slightly heightened. But the change was quick. It became out of control, panicked, and I could feel pain behind each breath.

Whatever I'd witnessed happening to him in the parking lot last week, something I thought maybe I'd imagined or read too much into, was happening to him again now. Which meant I hadn't imagined the incident in the parking lot at all. I'd seen something then just like I was hearing something now.

It terrified me.

I didn't know how to help.

Or how to react.

What to say.

What not to say.

If I should run and get help.

If I should stay near him.

I touched my hand to his back as gently as possible. I wanted to hug him, but I was afraid to—afraid he might push me away. But as I lay there feeling useless, I decided I had to try something. I moved to my knees, scooting closer to his body, and I leaned over him.

He didn't embrace my awkward hug, nor did he push me away. I hovered over him, digging my fingers into his arm, my heart racing all the while.

All I could think was *how many times had he suffered through one of these?* I wanted to ask, but my mouth wasn't able to form the words. A few minutes passed like this until finally something in him relaxed and his breathing slowed. Just like that, whatever it was, it lessened.

It occurred to me then that maybe I'd just violated his space when he was at his worst. Maybe he hadn't pushed me away because he was too paralyzed to push me away. Fuck. I began to move, but he caught my arm, not letting me leave.

"Stay," he muttered. "Stay, please."

My heart warmed at those simple words.

"Stay the night," he added.

The only thing his panic attack, if that was what he just had, made me feel was something greater for him. He seemed like such a strong, confident, controlled man. His appearance, his voice, his attitude, even his smile—it all oozed confidence. But I saw a crack in his outer surface, in his shell. I liked that crack. We all have cracks. Cracks make us human. I wanted to see under those cracks and get to know the Nick he so clearly kept buried underneath.

"I'll stay," I whispered.

I kept my place over him like a blanket. More time passed. Eventually my legs started to lose circulation. I had to move. I lay back against his sheets. He moved then, rolling over and into me. He squeezed his arms around my waist and pulled me firmly, flush up against his warm, solid body, my back to his chest.

"What happened just now?" I dared to ask.

"Don't," he whispered. "I don't want to talk about it. Just lay with me."

I swallowed.

I had a lot of questions, but I held them in as he held me tight. He ran his hands over my body. He moved a hand to my lower stomach. *Did he realize where he was putting his hand, what was there underneath his fingertips?*

It became obvious that he did realize, when he whispered, "It's a good thing our timing was off. It's a good thing the life inside you isn't mine. Mental illness, it can be genetic. Most days I feel like I'm fucking cursed. Either that, or just fucking crazy. Finn might not be the most intelligent human being in the world, but I'm sure genetically he's a much better bet than me for your future child."

"You can't really believe that," I argued. "And I don't mean about Finn." Who was actually a lot smarter than he looked.

"It's not a matter of belief; it's a matter of science. I've researched it. I know the numbers. There's almost a fifty percent chance any child of mine would also have Panic Disorder just like me. It's why I don't want kids of my own. But being part of someone else's kid's life... I could get behind that."

I breathed out.

That was a lot to take in. A lot to process.

"You're keeping it, right?" he wanted to know next.

"Yes. Why wouldn't I?" Tears burned in my eyes. No matter what

Nick carried in his genes, or thought he carried in his genes, there was no question about me keeping this child. I'd never give up my baby. I'd never give up his. I didn't really understand his panic attacks or what it was like for him during one. But they didn't seem like as much of a curse as he described. Not enough to not want his baby.

"Just a question," he whispered.

"Kind of a shitty question."

"Just a question," he repeated. "I didn't mean anything by it. I'm glad you're keeping the baby. You're going to be a great mother."

"I need sleep," I huffed. Because my skin felt itchy all of a sudden. He barely knew me. He didn't know if I'd make a good mother or a horrible mother. What was he building that statement on? My skills as a tattoo artist? My skills at fucking him that one time several weeks ago? Because, seriously, that was all he even knew about me. "We're strangers. You barely know me."

Nick let go of his grip around my middle. I pulled away from him and shifted over to the opposite side of his king-sized bed. I'd had so many highs and lows this evening. And now I was annoyed with him. We were both still in our underwear. But he didn't move to get out of bed and neither did I. I just lay there until I fell asleep. I'd process all this in the morning.

I knew now that I should have been honest with him from the start. I should have told him the baby was his. Of all the men in this world who might have reacted poorly, I now believed this particular man wouldn't have been one of them. But it was too late now. I couldn't take back what I'd said about Finn.

~ CHAPTER 21 ~

NICK

A moment alone in my own head, and I had this sneaking suspicion the baby was mine. I lay in the dark, I could hear Amanda's steady breaths, I knew she'd fallen asleep, and it was all I could think about.

She'd fallen asleep pissed at me. She'd overreacted to a simple question.

So much so that it had me wondering. Was the baby mine? I racked my brain trying to remember if we'd used a condom, and I concluded that we hadn't. That night Finn took off with some other woman, in a Jeep, and I wondered if I could find that woman. Working for the North Carolina Aquatic Preservation Society meant I often worked closely with the local police. In the morning maybe I'd call a police friend of mine to figure out how many black Jeep Grand Cherokees were registered in this one town. Maybe he could help me find her. Maybe finding that woman could help clarify more about Finn.

Or rather than going through all that, I could just ask Amanda. I knew that. But I didn't want to ask her. I liked her, but what did it say about her if she'd just lied about this baby?

She was this huge enigma—a sexy enigma—but still an enigma. I needed to figure her out before I accused her of something so big. I needed more time with her. She knew my secret now, about my panic attacks, and I kind of loved the way she'd reacted. She was affectionate rather than interrogative.

So I would try to be the same for her.

Eventually I got some sleep, but I woke up when I felt Amanda move closer to me. She poked my ribs. "I didn't like your question," she whispered into the pitch black. I couldn't see her face, but I felt the strain in her voice. "Have I thought about the thing you asked? Yes, but I already decided I would never do that, no matter what. At work everyone knows, and you weren't the first person to say those words—to ask if I planned on keeping it or not. Just because I don't have a plan or because I've never done this before, it doesn't mean that I can't do it. Or that I can't do it alone. It hurt me when you said that. I wish people would stop saying that. Or suggesting that."

She had my heart beating so hard. "Who else suggested it?"

"Nobody."

"Finn?"

"Maybe."

Fuck Finn. I rolled over closer to her. I would kick Finn's ass for this, for anything he might have suggested to her. But suddenly I realized how my words to her might have been construed. "I didn't mean to hurt you. I asked that because I wanted to make sure you were keeping the baby. Because I want you to. I want to do this with you. I'll be your plan, remember? More and more, you're becoming all I care about."

"Same," she whispered.

I don't know what happened, but I couldn't keep my hands off her after that. They went to her waist, and I yanked her over on top of me so that she was straddling my body. My breathing became wild. I needed this woman. Now.

I sat up to kiss her mouth. She was warm and accepting. I tasted saltiness in that kiss, like tears, and a rush of protectiveness ran through me.

She was scared.

I was scared.

But we were in this together. Whether the baby was mine or not.

I kept kissing her. I couldn't get enough. I wanted more. I needed more. She was right there with me because I felt her reach back to unhook her bra. She took it off and flung it aside. She grabbed my face, kissed against my ear, and she whispered, "Don't make me wait the entire night before we get to the good stuff this time. Please, Nick. Pregnancy hormones are a real thing. I need you to fuck me."

Wow. I was going to marry this woman.

Not even kidding.

She had my body vibrating with need. I smiled; I couldn't help it. I moved my hands to her breasts, squeezing them gently, moving my thumbs over her nipples, playing with her. Her nipples were hard little points, and I fucking loved it. I put my mouth to skin, dragging my tongue against her, tasting her.

"Nick," she moaned. "More."

But she was a drug, like morphine. I was dizzy, I was so lost in this girl. I moved my hands lower, needing to feel more of her. I touched her slick warmth. Then I pressed a finger deep inside her. Oh God, she was wet and warm and the noise she made when I touched her made me forget about everything else in the world. Nothing mattered but this woman. "More?" I whispered.

"Yes," she breathed. "Nick, I need more."

During our first time together, the reason I focused on foreplay all night, was because I was trying to be good, trying to be a gentleman, trying to give off the same persona I always did. The 'good guy' persona. I don't know why it was so deeply engrained into me. But even then, in the end, I hadn't been able to keep up that facade with her.

Not much was different this time.

In fact, the shell slipped up twice as easily and twice as fast this time. I hardly gave a fuck. She moved to work off her underwear, and I moved to work off mine. Then, a spilt second later, I pushed inside her. I held her at her waist, guiding her on top of me.

Nothing had ever felt this good. She was my muse, my weakness, my hope. Something animalistic took over. I got out of my own head. I stopped worrying about every little thing, and I just enjoyed her.

~ CHAPTER 22 ~

AMANDA

"Nick! Oh God, yes, Nick!" I moaned into his shoulder. I bit down against his flesh, trying to stifle my screams, not wanting his roommate to hear me.

Nick did most of the work. He moved me, his hands at my waist, up and down against his hard length. Good thing because I had become complete gelatin. He felt so good inside me, filling me, stretching me. This man knew how to fuck. But this wasn't a surprise, I already knew this about him. I knew it the moment he first smiled at me. Something about the little smirk that was always there on his lips gave it away.

And boy, did I ever feel it now. He was relentless, moving me hard against his body, grinding at just the right angle.

I lost control.

I was at his mercy.

Along for the ride.

I was his completely in the moment.

Sharp electricity zapped through me as he brought me to yet another orgasm. I squeezed my arms around his neck harder. "Nick! Yes!" I cried out. He pumped harder. His fingers at my hips were going to leave bruises. I didn't care. He felt way too good. The tingles moving all through me—way too good. His warm body moving with mine—way too good.

We were both lost in each other. A second later, he came inside me. He slowed and I felt his release. He hadn't used a condom. This time, I guess it didn't matter.

Out of breath, completely spent, I flopped onto the bed beside him. Silently, we both lay together, side by side. He tugged me closer, against his slightly sweaty chest, and dammit if my heart didn't pound even harder. I liked him. A lot. And little by little, I felt like I was surrendering more of myself to this guy I barely knew.

That was almost as terrifying as carrying his baby. I knew I would need to do something to protect myself from the inevitable heartbreak a guy like this could cause. But not right this minute. Right this minute I didn't care much.

I simply sighed against his chest. Then I let myself fall asleep breathing in his fresh scent.

The moment sunshine hit my eyelids, I awoke, and I slipped out of bed. Not making a sound, I stared down at a sleeping Nick. The guy was all man. Buck-ass naked. Sprawled out on top of the covers like he didn't give a fuck. Men in real life—they didn't look like this guy. They didn't smell like him. They didn't taste like him. They just weren't real. And when one of them did come along, they were always, always too good to be true.

So this guy... was this guy for real?

I found my underwear and bra on the floor. I worked quietly to slip them on.

This guy, I decided, couldn't be the exception to the rule. Not a chance the exception to the rule would pick me out of the crowd. He was saying all the right things. Or at least most of the right things. And I was having an impossible time believing him right this second in the light of day.

Case in point, Emma Winchester. His ex-girlfriend. I could picture him and sweet, angelic Emma Winchester together. They were like a Hallmark card. What about me? If Emma was a Hallmark card, I was a spiral notebook paper with poorly drawn doodles.

"You're awake," he muttered, startling me from my thoughts. His eyes were closed but somehow, he'd caught me. "Get back in bed."

"No. I need to go." He'd driven me to his house last night. I was stuck. "I'm going to go find my clothes in the bathroom. Will you drive me home after?"

He made a noise deep in his throat, sleepy and sexy. "Lou's probably been in there already. She's probably washed and folded them and placed them somewhere around the house—like the way a cat would leave a dead mouse on a doorstep. I try not to leave anything anywhere. Let me get up. Let me go find your clothes."

I waited for him to get up.

He didn't move. For a second, I thought he'd fallen back to sleep. "Nick," I whispered. "Please, I need to go."

His eyes finally cracked opened. He squinted in the sun. His eyes were such a sharp, beautiful aqua blue color in the morning sun that they stung me—literally stung.

"Hi," he muttered, giving me that charming smirk of his . "Hi. Good morning."

"Hi."

God. I couldn't help it. I felt giddy. I felt excited to see him stare up at me. He sat up, swung his legs over the edge of the bed, rubbed at his eyes, and then ultimately left the bed. This man was so amazingly sexy padding around his room, barefoot, naked, and not at all worried that I was watching. He bumped into me as he moved past, on purpose, shooting me his smile that was going to be my undoing. He grabbed some fresh clothes from his dresser. He yanked on a shirt, underwear, sweats—even stumbling to get into a pair of socks. He kept digging around for more clothes.

He handed me some items. A sweatshirt for me to wear and some kind of running pants. "Here. Wear mine. I'll get your clothes back to you another day."

I paused for a moment but decided to put on the clothes he offered. Once I was dressed, I really melted. He was so low key, so kind, so go-with-the-flow. Another day? Did that mean he wanted a repeat of last night? Multiple repeats? Were the events from last night going to become a thing?

Maybe I wanted lots of repeats.

Maybe I didn't.

I couldn't decide.

We left his house. I never saw Lou—or my clothes—on the way out. I rode with him in his car. "You hungry?" he asked when we passed a couple of fast food places on the way. "Want me to stop somewhere?" He scratched at the stubble on his face. He looked good with that stubble.

I was starving. But I couldn't keep asking for him to do more for me.

"I'm okay."

"You want to come over to my place again tonight? I could pick you up again. Or you could just drive over after work." He reached the *Kill Devil Ink* parking lot. He pulled into a spot beside a car that wasn't mine; it was Finn's actually, but I didn't think Nick knew that. Good.

"Maybe. I'll think about it," I muttered, unbuckling. I opened my door before I let the situation become awkward, before he leaned in for a kiss, or before I gave in and told him how crazy about him I really was.

I needed space.

I needed to think.

~ CHAPTER 23 ~

NICK

It was early, six in the morning early. I dropped Amanda off in front of *Kill Devil Ink.* Surely, at this hour, she didn't need to be at work. There were only two cars in the lot, the same two cars as the night we'd first been together. I thought she'd leave my car and get into one of the parked cars.

She went into the building instead.

Finn—*fucking Finn*—opened the front door for her. Fuck him. I saw him through the glass. He saw me too. I resisted the urge to flip him off; instead I waved and drove away.

Seeing her go to him, go inside with him, it hit me like a punch in the stomach. There was nothing out of the ordinary about it, but for as convinced as I'd had myself all night that the baby was mine, now I wasn't convinced at all.

Jesus, did I want to do this even if the baby wasn't mine? I could support Amanda as her friend. I'd always be her friend. But should I leave it at that and step aside?

Damn. I gripped the steering wheel tighter. I did not want to be her friend. I reached my driveway and I lingered in the car for a minute. The image of her pale pink hair, all wild and crazy in the morning, the first thing I saw when I opened my eyes, was clouding all my thoughts. My breathing started to speed.

Fuck—*not again.*

I did not need to deal with another panic attack. They were happening way too frequently lately. I jumped out of the car and I took off running. I ran at full speed. I ran and I ran. My body didn't have time to panic and shut down, it had time only for running.

Eventually I looped around the neighborhood and came back to the house. As I slowed, I felt better. Somehow, I'd curbed what might have been another attack. Lou scared me half to death, though. I found her sitting on the front lawn, waiting on me.

"Oh my gosh," she cried out, jumping to her feet. "Your girlfriend is pregnant and the father is Finn, the hot tattoo artist!" She had a smile on her face as she yelled this at me. Like it was good news.

Dripping sweat, out of breath from my run, I walked over to her. I started stretching out my hamstrings. "You were listening."

"Of course I was listening. I mean, I listened to your dinner conversation. That's all I heard. I didn't hear anything else."

"You're outside the house."

"I know." She bounced her feet on the dewy, sandy grass that was our front yard. She stood there when I'd never seen her venture this far outside any building on her own. "The grass is soft and not so scary."

It was prickly and mostly weeds. More and more lately I questioned if Lou had real agoraphobia. Perhaps, all these years, she'd only convinced herself she had it. Honestly, she'd seen me have about a million panic attacks, and I'd never once seen her have one of her own. She talked about having them. And maybe she used to have them occasionally. But I wondered when was the last time that she *actually* had one of her own.

Not that that was a bad thing.

That was a *very* good thing.

I just wondered if it wasn't time to start pushing her out into the world more. Maybe she'd find out she wasn't half as broke as she always believed.

"The baby is definitely yours, if that's what you're thinking," she added, still smiling.

"She told me it was Finn's," I countered. Maybe I should be grounding myself in reality, not hoping for some alternative I'd created in my mind last night.

"It's not Finn's."

"How do you know that?" I shouted at her. I ran my hands through my damp hair, frustrated as hell.

"The day we got your hat. She stared at you like she'd seen a ghost. Or maybe like she'd seen her baby's father walking back in through the front door when she'd thought she'd never see him again. She kept your hat as a souvenir. She knew the baby was yours then. She knew it when she came over last night. She knows it. You're the dad. Case closed."

I stood there, staring at Lou with my mouth hanging open. The thing about Lou was—she was really smart. She'd read every book she could get her hands on when she lived in the library. She taught herself my coursework right alongside me while I was in college. She should have the same degree as me. She'd also spied on thousands of teenagers, like watching daily on-going soap operas, and I believed she had a gift when it came to reading people.

"Why would she lie?"

"I don't know. She's scared? She's a pathological liar? Who knows?"

I gave her a look. That wasn't really helpful. "Now what?"

"You should probably take a shower. You're dripping sweat onto the grass. Ew."

"No, I mean now what with Amanda?"

"Well, your last girlfriend thought you were boring. So you should probably show this girl that you *aren't*."

I breathed in deeply. "Okay. Thanks for that reminder. Not sure how to prove to someone I'm not boring, but okay."

"Nick," she said with complete sincerity. "You are definitely *not* boring."

~ CHAPTER 24 ~

AMANDA

"Wait, let me get this straight?" Finn shook his head at me. "You told him I was the father? Why?"

"It seemed like a good idea at first. Like a way to test the waters. He reacted really well to the news, actually, and I spent the night with him last night. But, I'm starting to get this sense that Nick is really good at playing the parts he plays."

"What do you mean?"

"Like a person who goes to extremes to please everyone else. Like he hides a lot of who he is. Anyway, I'm going to take off. Get home. Get showered. I'll see you later though. Have a good morning."

"Bye, Amanda. I hope you know what you're doing."

"Yeah, me too."

I left the shop, pushing open the double doors. I sure as hell hoped I knew what I was doing. Good sense told me to keep some distance from Nick, for now anyway. But the other half of me wanted none of that. The other half wanted to dive head first, all in, with Nick. I couldn't decide which part of myself to trust. Cautious me or carefree me? After all, it was carefree me who slept with a stranger and got me into this mess in the first place.

I went home, I went on with my day, and I tried not to think of Nick at all. I returned to the shop around noon, when I was due to start my work day, and I kept busy so there wasn't too much time to stop and think about him. I even managed to stay late. I took an additional customer when I could have turned them away. By the time I left, it was late. Way past dinnertime.

I hadn't texted Nick. I didn't have his number to text him. But I wouldn't have either way. I decided it was better to not see him two days in a row.

Except, as I started driving home—*shit!*—I missed my turn. I kept going. I kept driving. My mind was screaming at me to turn around, to go home, to leave things alone for now. But dammit, my hands and my feet didn't comply.

I drove straight to Nick's house.

Then I sat in my car for a while, like a complete crazy person, trying to convince myself to turn around and head home.

Eventually, I left my car. My heart was racing like mad. What was I doing? My stomach was in knots. I climbed the wooden stairs that led me to the deck attached to the second level of his house.

I didn't go to the front door.

I went to the sliding glass door connected to his room. I knocked softly on the glass. It was after ten. This was insanity. What would I even say when he opened the glass door—*if* he opened the glass door?

It took him a second, but he appeared at the glass. He moved the curtain, saw me, and unlocked the door. Once he slid it open, I squeezed through the opening, so that I was close to him. So close I could smell him. He smelled so freaking amazing—like mint and pine. Immediately my whole body felt a bit dizzy. His hands found my waist in the pale light.

"I don't really want to talk," I whispered.

"We don't have to talk."

He pressed his lips to my neck.

They were like heaven on my skin. Soft and warm. He snaked his arms around my body, tugging me closer. But I softly pushed at his chest to make him stop. "I actually just want to sleep."

He pulled back, and I stared up at him. Every ounce of me was longing for something comfortable. And his bed last night had been so damn comfortable. His body, his touch—the very definition of comfortable. It was why I couldn't keep myself away from him tonight. That comfort. That need. I worried for a moment he wouldn't want me to stay if it was only for sleep.

"Then we should sleep," he said, surprising me. He tugged at my hand, pulling me toward his bed. I kicked off my shoes as I moved across his room with him. I followed him into bed, curling next to him under the covers. Today had been easier. I'd kept my meals down. And now this, tucked close to him, was a cherry on top of a really good day.

His smell was intoxicating. Breathing him in made my body warm and my thoughts go a little fuzzy. How easy would it be to kiss him and get lost in the moment again, like last night?

But I pulled away from his body. I moved over to the other side of his bed. "Goodnight, Nick," I whispered, flipping over to my side, my back to him now, wrapping my arms around one of his pillows.

"Goodnight," he returned.

He sounded a little confused. Maybe even a little hurt.

I wanted so desperately to stay curled next to him. Worse still, sleep wasn't the only thing my body wanted. I wanted to feel him inside me again. I wanted the rush I knew he could give me. I even wanted to say something, anything, even just to tell him all about my day. But I didn't. I lay still. I fought every impulse that came my way.

This was better. Safer.

I could test out how I felt for him at a distance. I needed to protect myself. Because sex with this man felt way too fucking good. Conversations, almost too natural. His smiles, not easy on my heart. Even his mattress—way too damn heavenly.

I couldn't let myself have it all.

I couldn't let myself fall.

If I let myself have it all, I'd be at his mercy. That wasn't a position, especially when I had a child to worry about now, that I wanted to leave myself in.

Keeping a safe distance felt like my only option.

~ CHAPTER 25 ~

NICK

Eight days.

For eight days straight Amanda showed up at my house, same time, same way, and slept in my bed with me. She started coming in with wet hair. Her face free of makeup. Her pajamas already on. Like she'd been home, showered, prepared for bed, and at the last second decided to come sleep next to me.

We weren't talking.

We weren't fucking.

I wasn't entirely sure what this was or what this meant. I liked it, though, I really did. I liked hearing her breathing at night, having her in my bed, knowing she'd always show up at a certain time.

I wanted to ask questions. But I didn't.

She kept me at arm's length. And so I kept her at arm's length. Was this Emma Winchester all over again? This weird, half-relationship, where I stuck around way too long, hoping for more, hoping for some clarity, and never got any?

I had no idea.

But for all the words we weren't saying, there was something else. Sideways looks. Small smiles.

Anything she did, it seemed, could make my heart race. She sat on the edge of my bed this morning, tying her shoes. "Would you like to go to dinner tonight?"

She breathed the words rather than spoke them. Seriously, she hadn't said more than a 'goodnight' or a 'goodbye' to me in eight days. I sat up in bed. Hell yes, I wanted to go.

"It's a work thing," she explained. "It's not mandatory or anything. Once a month John, my boss... you know, the guy who caught us naked that morning." *The morning I got her pregnant? It wasn't like I'd forgotten.* "He invites everyone out once a month. He pays. It's nice. It's casual. Actually, I think his wife is behind it. We're allowed to invite an extra, a significant other or friend to come with. You know."

"John Michaels is married?"

This was the shocker of the century. I knew of John, her boss, originally through Emma. And now through Amanda. He was cold and quiet. Not the 'married, white-picket-fence' type in any way. How did that even happen?

"He's married to Dani Mills. She's Caleb Mill's cousin. Caleb Mills of *Sunset Revival*. Dani is the drummer of the band."

Well, fuck. Caleb Mills blew into town and stole away Emma... what, nine months ago? Maybe ten? How in that time had John Michaels, the most standoff-ish guy, landed and married Dani Mills? She was as famous as Caleb. Everyone knew who she was.

"Yeah, I'll go to dinner," I said.

"You realize there's a possibility that Emma and Caleb could be at this thing." She turned around to look at me from her spot on the end of the bed, her eyes meeting mine. Her fingers were still on the laces of one shoe even though I think she was done tying it.

She was so pretty. Her hair was a wavy, pink mane framing her face. Her shirt clung tight over her chest. She wasn't wearing a bra, and I could almost see her nipples through her shirt. We hadn't spoken in eight days, but we were speaking now, and I couldn't get enough of it. "I hope not. But it wouldn't stop me from going with you. Does everyone at your work know? About the baby, I mean, about it being Finn's?"

She turned back around. Her back to me again. "Yeah. They know."

"And they know... about you and I? This." Whatever *this* was.

"Yeah."

I didn't know what she was telling people. It occurred to me then, whether I was the father or not, she was probably discussing all of this with everyone *but* me. Finn included.

How could I show her that she could trust me? That she could talk to me about everything, lean on me the most, depend on me, let me be the person she confided in.

"Just tell me when and where. I'll be there. I can pick you up and drive if you'd like. Actually, I'd really like to show up that way. Not meet there."

"Yeah." She stood from the edge of the bed. "Here." She went to my nightstand. I had a pad of paper and a pencil there. When I used to have nightmares, writing down the details of each incident on paper had helped me overcome them. I still kept the paper there, even though it had been a couple years since my last one.

She wrote down her address. She didn't meet my eyes while she did this.

"Okay I have to go."

She turned for the sliding glass door, about to take off and sneak away just like she did every morning. A blur and she'd be gone.

"Amanda," I called after her. I hopped out of bed, realizing just how badly I wanted more than whatever limbo we—*she*—had stuck us in. I went to the sliding glass door, standing next to her before she made her escape. "Thanks for inviting me. I'm good with people, I promise. Really good with stuff like this. With or without an ex in the audience."

Her eyes moved to mine. She kind of squinted at me like she was trying to figure me out. "Okay. Bye, Nick," she said.

She slid open the door. Not commenting on what I'd just said, not lingering for a kiss or anything like that. Then she disappeared just the same as any other morning.

~ CHAPTER 26 ~

AMANDA

In my entire life, I don't think I'd ever been this nervous. I changed my outfit eighteen times as I got ready, finally settling on a jean skirt, leggings, and a cutoff t-shirt. This dinner thing was always casual. No one would be dressed up.

So I couldn't show up with him looking like I was trying too hard. But also, I wanted to look different when Nick saw me again. The only times he ever saw was me ready for bed: no makeup, pajamas, in the dark as I snuck into his bed each night. It was my own fault, I know, but tonight I wanted him to see something more.

I did my makeup.

I did my nails and my hair. I scrubbed and shaved practically every inch of my body. I used my favorite lotion, a discontinued brand I only had a little bit of left, that I saved for the really special occasions. I wasn't sure what justified this as one of those moments. But I'd used some of that lotion just for this. Just for him.

There was a knock as I was finishing my marathon of pampering. My heart stampeded as I grabbed my bag and my shoes, and hurried for the door. I opened it, rushed outside in my bare feet, and pretty much collided right into his body as I pulled the door shut with me. I didn't want him seeing inside. My house, which used to be Dad's house, was about three times smaller than his rental. My house was lived in, pretty old, and nothing worth showing off. I kept it clean, but I don't think clean was impressive when you'd grown up with money.

"Hi," I muttered, staring up at him. He had his hat on. The same knit hat he'd left behind that first night. It was a warm evening, he didn't need a hat, but he sure looked damn good in it.

I dropped to the cement. He took a small step back. Unlike so many of the houses built purposely one story off the ground in the Outer Banks. My house was ground level. It was older than me and still standing. I worked at slipping on my heels with the cold slab of cement against my ass.

He knelt down close to me, his elbows on his knees. His blue eyes were on mine. "How are you?"

"I'm good." I worked on the buckle of my shoes. They were strappy and cute, possibly a little past casual. But when else did I ever get chances to wear shoes that weren't sneakers? The buckle was being stubborn, though.

He touched my hair and I paused. I'd blown it out and curled it into big waves, and it was kind of wild. The curls would not hold, but for now I knew it looked great. He fingered a strand, swirling his thumb against the pink.

"I can't get enough of you," he said, smiling. That smile—the kind that could make a girl tingle in places involuntarily. I wasn't immune and today it was especially cocky on his lips. He touched my shoe. I hadn't figured out the buckle, and for a moment I thought he might have been kneeling down to help me, when instead he pushed my right one off my foot.

Then my left.

I took a breath and crossed my legs, barefoot now on my front porch. "What are you doing?"

He moved his hands to my knees. Hovering closer, he leaned in to whisper, "Wanting more."

He gave my thighs a little squeeze, his eyes moving back to look into mine, his mouth way too close to mine now.

My chest was on fire.

He softly kissed the corner of my mouth. "You dressed up for me."

"I didn't. I always dress like this."

He made a noise in his throat. Then he started kissing me more, slow kisses across my jaw line. It felt so nice. I rested my weight back on my hands, letting him kiss my jaw then my neck.

"You're lying," he muttered.

"Fine," I whispered. "I dressed up for you."

He pulled back. I must have satisfied him with that answer because he was about to stand up, to pull away, but I suddenly found myself also wanting more. I grabbed his neck and pushed my lips into his. He continued to pull back. "Come here," he muttered, grabbing my hand, helping me stand.

My bare feet were on the cement now. I stood there with him, my emotions zigzagging all over the place. From nervous to annoyed to hopeful to scared. He tugged off his beanie, holding it in his hands. His hair underneath was messy, but on him, impossible to look bad.

He touched gently under my chin, his hat still in hand, tipping my face up toward him. "Come here," he muttered right before...

He kissed me.

Oh God, did he kiss me.

His hands moved to the sides of my face, and he pressed those soft, warm lips of his against mine. I felt his tongue. I was hooked on his tongue. It was a slow, savory kiss. And dammit, if it wasn't the best of my life.

I don't know why the kiss I'd tried to start on the floor hadn't been good enough—why he'd made me stand and then taken his hat off for this. Why this kiss suddenly beat out all his other kisses. I mean, his other ones in the past had been great and all, toe-curling even, but this one made something inside me scream.

I melted into him, wrapping my arms around his torso, feeling the width and strength of his back. He smelled like heaven, tasted like heaven—he *was* heaven.

Another minute later, he broke the kiss. He tugged on his hat, smiling all cocky at me. "Come on, let's go to dinner." He cleared his throat as he spoke, his voice hoarse and rough, thanks to our mind-blowing kiss.

I felt dizzy. I couldn't even speak. My body was buzzing, my heart was thumping, and I had no idea what he'd just done to me. "Yeah," I muttered. I bent to my knees, once again about to attempt getting these strappy shoes on my feet. But then quickly decided I didn't care about wearing heels. "You know what, fuck it," I mumbled to myself.

I kicked the heels behind, close to my front door. Inside my bag, I grabbed my keys to unlock it. Just inside the door, I had the sneakers I always wore. Only cracking the door a minimal amount, I reached in and grabbed them.

I slipped them on instead.

I don't think Nick cared what was on my feet, I decided. The guy was still around even when he thought I had Finn's baby inside me. Shoes seemed trivial in comparison. He was here despite everything else. It made me realize, for the first time, just how much he liked me.

~ CHAPTER 27 ~

NICK

"There was this one time my mom told me not to touch the oven stovetop when it was red, because that meant it was hot, so I made direct eye contact with her and slapped my hand down on the burner."

We were at dinner. There were only eight of us altogether. Somehow in my mind I'd imagined this would involve a larger group. When we'd arrived, a little late, the others had already been seated at the table. Only two open seats were left. On the end. Across from one another. I took one of the seats next to a guy named Patrick. Amanda sat across from me. Right next to none other than Finn himself. He immediately put his hand up to his face, and whispered something to her. Something that made her smile for a second.

Christ, fucking help me.

Where was his plus one? He didn't have one.

Patrick didn't have a girlfriend with him either. He kept poking at me, trying to make small, side conversation with me. I wanted none of it. And I immediately went into 'crowd pleaser Nick' mode, talking to the whole table as if I didn't have serious underlying issues with anxiety.

That story about the hand on the burner wasn't even my story. It was Mick's. My brother was the lovable rebel type, the kind of a guy with a million good stories from childhood. I had none of those defining type stories of my own. I was a good kid, the kind who listened to his mom when she said the stove was hot, but that sort of thing made for boring conversation.

Growing up with parents who were so involved in the community meant I had to deal with dinners and social situations all the time. When I gained a brother, I gained a model, and he showed me that there was a way to navigate these types of things, and it was with comedy and complete bullshit. Mick used to encourage me to use whatever story I wanted of his to help me when I was most anxious. He grew up in a trailer park, so he had an endless supply of entertaining stories.

Everyone at the table laughed. Even John Michaels laughed. Amanda didn't fully smile though. She did have her eyes on me, watching me. It felt like she was trying to dissect me.

"So you're from Maine?" Finn asked. The waitress was down at the other end of the table, taking orders, so I no longer had the whole table's attention. "What's that like?"

I crossed my arms, resting them on the table, shrugging. We weren't friends, a million miles from it, but he was being awfully friendly all of a sudden. "It's fine. You have to take a ferry to get to where my parents live. Peaks Island. So it's secluded. Parts of it remind me of here. Except with much colder winters."

"What do your parents do?"

"My dad makes custom furniture. He has a company in Portland. My mom runs the business side of it. They're a good team."

"And you have a brother?"

"Yes. He's a professional baseball player."

"Well, that's cool. You go to college?"

"Yes."

"Where?"

"Boston."

"Boston what?"

"Boston University."

"When you say professional baseball player, do you mean like major league?"

"Yes. That's what I meant."

"Oh, okay. Wow."

Finn was asking more questions than, I swear to God, any girlfriend or date of mine ever had. What the hell did that say about me? About him? Unless... unless these questions weren't his questions at all, but instead Amanda's questions for me. She was about the only reason I answered each one of them easily and truthfully.

His line of questions came to a halt because it was my time to order from our waitress.

"Hey, sugar," the woman said to me. She was young. She was pretty. She touched my arm. This was the flirtation of the south, apparently. Finn asked about the differences between here and where I grew up, and sometimes I couldn't tell if people were in my space, just like this waitress with her hand on my arm, because that was normal friendliness around here, or for other reasons.

"I'll just have the Cobb salad, thanks."

She bent over to whisper against my ear. "You look like a movie star, baby. What are you doing with these folks?"

I didn't answer. I only politely smiled at her as she pulled away, not interested, instead handing her my menu. I guess, this time, it wasn't just friendliness. She walked away after that, finished with all of our orders.

When I looked back at Amanda her cheeks were a little flushed. I wasn't interested in the waitress, I hoped that was easy to see.

The rest of the meal wasn't very eventful. Amanda and I didn't speak. Finn made more forced conversation with me. Same with Patrick. All of it very civil. A lot of it sports related. Once people knew my brother was a professional athlete, that was usually where the conversation strayed.

My eyes kept coming back to Amanda's. I wasn't here for conversation about baseball. I wasn't here to make friends with her friends. I was here for her. Finally, the ordeal ended. Dinner was over. It was time to go.

I realized then how fucking awful it really had been. Painfully... boring. Another meal with a woman who probably could have been napping through it all the same. My stomach felt hollow. It made me tug on Amanda's hand as everyone else was walking away.

As they all left out the door, I held her back. "Stay," I muttered.

"What?"

"Let's stay and have a drink at the bar."

"I'm pregnant."

"Right." *Obviously. I was an idiot.* "Let's stay and have dessert then."

"I'd rather get key lime pie at the place just down the street. We could walk. It isn't too far."

"Perfect." Anything to redeem myself. I had to redeem myself. We left together, walking away from the building in the opposite direction, toward the place with the key lime pie she mentioned. It was a nice night. Just the walk alone, even along the side of the street with cars passing us by, was better already for me than the whole dinner had been.

Why couldn't I be normal?

Why couldn't I just talk to her?

Why did I have to feel anxious all the time?

~ CHAPTER 28 ~

AMANDA

"**T**his pie is the best, right?" I said to Nick, hoping it made up for everything crappy about that dinner. He was such a gentleman through it all—talking to everyone, joking with everyone, answering every one of the questions Finn grilled him with, talking baseball with the guys when part of me got the impression baseball wasn't even an interest of his.

And the waitress. God, she wouldn't leave him alone. She kept petting his arm, literally petting him like a dog, every time she walked by. I was so embarrassed. He had to have been annoyed by the entire thing. Annoyed with me for inviting him. Annoyed with all of us for being... so basic. We were a group of tattoo artists; I'd never really thought of any of us as basic before, but that was before I learned as much as I learned about Nick tonight from all of Finn's incessant questioning.

At one point, I excused myself and went to the bathroom. I googled him like a fucking fanatic in the closed stall. I googled his brother. Red Sox player. His parents. Owners of some fancy, custom-made furniture company. Peaks Island. His hometown. An island full of the most impressive mansions I'd ever laid my eyes on. An island for the rich, it seemed. His college, super prestigious, and apparently one of the best marine biology programs in the country.

He was a silver spoon baby.

A millionaire's son.

He made conversation easily with all of us regular people. And he was good at it. So nice when put on the spot. It shocked me a little that he wanted to have dessert with me, that he wanted to keep this evening going.

Because he had to be reconsidering being with me, entertaining me, staying around when he still believed me to be pregnant with Finn's baby.

Oh God, what would his parents think if he told them he was dating a pregnant girl? They'd probably both have heart attacks. I didn't know them at all. But I could imagine it. Were we even dating? Just occasionally... casually... fucking. And me tactlessly showing up to sleep in his bed each night. He probably would never dare tell his family about me.

"This is the best pie I've ever had," he said to me. "I normally don't like key lime pie."

I gave him a small smile. "Me neither."

"We should have eaten here for dinner." He took another bite. "Alone," he added. "It's just I turn into this weird version of myself around other people. This Chaz."

Chaz? He had my heart pounding hard. "What's a Chaz?"

"A dick. My parents forced me to attend so many social events growing up. I developed this kind of alter ego."

"And Chaz is what you call your dick-ish alter ego?" I raised my eyebrows.

He set down his fork, turning over his hand. "That story about the burner and my hand was bullshit."

"What?" I glanced down at his hand. I could see no scars. So he'd made up that story where he slapped the burner completely. He'd done it so easily, so effortlessly. What else had he told everyone that wasn't true? "Boston College?" I asked. "Did you even go to school there?"

"No, I went there. The key to bullshitting people is to tell eighty percent of the honest truth, and another twenty percent embellished truth. My brother was the one who slapped the burner. And it was when he first came to live with us and was in this power struggle with my mom. The Chaz version of myself isn't me at all." He tugged off his hat, tossing it aside on the table, running a hand through his hair. "I like you, Amanda. I like you, but you need to know I'm not normal. I don't know how to be normal. Or more exciting, for that matter. The real me is a man with panic disorder who wears a beanie when it's one-hundred degrees outside and tries to pass it off as fashion. I don't want to bore you to death the way I did with Emma. I put her to sleep once. At dinner, she literally fell asleep on me one evening. Right at the fucking table. Sorry, I'm either the Chaz version of myself or the put-you-to-sleep version."

He took out his wallet and pulled out a few bills. Wait, was that it? We'd only been in this restaurant for a grand total of ten minutes. Now he was ready to go? I wished I wasn't pregnant because a few drinks together right now might be just what was needed.

"I want more pie," I practically shouted at him as he started to stand. "I'm not done. I'm eating for two. Don't rush me, please."

He was so freaking polite. He put the dollars back in his wallet just as fast as he'd pulled them out to leave.

And he sat back down.

"Fuck," I said to him, shaking my head. "I'm not really hungry still. I'm doing this thing where I eat tiny meals all day, so I don't vomit. My doctor suggested it for the morning sickness I'm having. As long as my stomach never gets fully empty, and I don't eat too much, I don't get nauseated. So no more pie for me. But you, I just want more of you. All versions please. Even Chaz. That's a terrible nickname for yourself, by the way. Terrible. Can we call your alter ego for yourself anything else?"

That elicited a smile on this handsome man's lips. "What do you have in mind?"

"Brad?"

He laughed out loud. He got my sarcasm. Brad was equally as bad as Chaz. He reached for his hat and he tugged it back on. "You're good at that," he commented.

"At what?" *What was his hat about? Part of his Chaz persona?* Now I wondered. I wondered why he liked to wear it all the time, even when it was warm.

"At making me smile." He reached across the table and he touched a strand of my hair, similar to the way he had on my porch. "I always smile twice as much when I'm with you. Sometimes my cheeks hurt because you make me smile so hard."

"We should go now," I muttered. I was feeling flushed, a little dizzy, and a whole lot of lust for this man. That was hands down one of the sweetest things any man had ever said to me.

Who the hell was he?

Really. Not Chaz. Not Emma's boring ex. Not some random customer anymore. Freaking A—I was crushing hard on this guy. All his strangeness and randomness only made him more attractive to me. And right now, I wanted back in his bed. Only, I didn't want to keep to my side tonight.

~ CHAPTER 29 ~

NICK

Amanda came home with me. She rode in my car. She walked up the wooden stairs, rather than sneaking in the sliding glass doors in the back to my room, and she stood with me while I unlocked the front door. "You need to meet Lou," I muttered to Amanda. Then louder, into the house, I shouted, "Lou! I'm back!"

Because Lou was home.

She was always home.

I wanted to give her a warning so she could either run to her room or prepare for Amanda coming in through the door.

She must have run to her room. Because Amanda and I walked inside, and Lou wasn't in the living room. I brought home a slice of key lime pie in a to-go box for her. I bet she'd never tried key lime before in her life. I grabbed a pen in the kitchen, wrote Lou's name on it, and shoved it in the fridge. She'd find it later.

Amanda sat down at one of the kitchen barstools. Her stomach was still just as flat as the day I met her. I wondered how long before her body would start to show the pregnancy. Suddenly, thoughts about the baby being Finn's crept into my mind.

One minute I'd be convinced—*absolutely convinced*—the baby was mine. Then the next all these doubts would come slipping into my brain. What if she hadn't lied? What if it was Finn's? I wanted to have the same attitude about the baby, about helping her after it came, regardless of whether or not I was the father. But to be honest, despite the way I'd always felt about having a child of my own, about fearing any kid of mine would have panic disorder like me, I wanted the baby to be mine so damn bad. I guess, the more time that passed where I didn't know with absolutely certainty it was mine, the more I began to believe it wasn't.

"Let's go to bed," I said to her.

I was stuck in my head, my emotions running all over the place, and I wanted her as a distraction before I ended up having a panic attack instead.

She followed me down the hall, back to my room. I flipped on the light, closing the door behind us. She gave me a small smile, touching my arm, and she walked deeper into my room. She took off her shoes, leaving them by my dresser where she always left them when she came in. She tugged off her skirt and the leggings she'd worn tonight, dropping them both to the floor.

Then in her shirt and just her underwear, she crawled into my bed. The way she smiled at me...

Wow.

What a fucking invitation that was.

"I need to, um, use the bathroom. I'll be back in a minute," I muttered, fumbling with my words. Then I left. Shit, any sane man would have been in bed with such a beautiful, sexy woman, inside her, making love to her body, in two seconds flat without a care in the world. Not me. I was out of the room and up the stairs that led to the top level only seconds later.

At Lou's door, I knocked softly.

"Lou, it's me. Just me. Can we talk?"

Lou cracked the door open only an inch wide. I saw one of her pale blue eyes through the small crack. "What?"

"How confident are you about the baby being mine?" I whispered to her. "How confident are you that it isn't Finn's? Like on a scale of one to ten. Ten being the most confident. What made you so certain that day in our yard?"

"What?" she said to me, not giving me even two inches of space to talk to her. "How was dinner?"

"Boring. Fine. Finn was there. He talked to me like we weren't enemies."

"Maybe you aren't."

"Bullshit. He's probably just as full of shit as I am. He probably only asked me all the polite questions that he asked because he's Amanda's friend. Or maybe, more likely, because he's in love with her too, and wanted to seem like a nice person. I don't really know. It just occurred to me that he probably knows her much better than I do. He probably knows how to make her scream about a million fucking times better than me. You know, given their 'casual sexual relationship'. Probably used to screw all the time at work, I would imagine. And he probably is the fucking father because why would she lie? Why would she lie about that to me?"

"Where is Amanda now? Did she go home?"

"No, she's in my bed. She's waiting for me."

"Okay, first of all... thanks for that visual of Finn making her scream. I didn't need that in my head. Second of all, you said the word *'probably'* about fifty times just now. Third, you said, *'in love with her too,'* implying you love her as well as Finn. Go be with your girlfriend. Go cuddle your girlfriend. Stop talking to me. She has the answers to your questions. I don't."

Lou closed the door.

She actually closed the door on me.

Did I say that? *In love with her too.*

Christ, I had said that. Now my heart was racing right out of my chest. Part of me considered sinking to the floor outside Lou's bedroom, riding out the panic attack I could feel was coming at me full force. But I didn't stay in the hallway.

I hurried back to my room. Back to Amanda.

I tossed my hat on the floor, flipped off the light, and I moved into bed with her. "I'm freaking the fuck out," I said to her in all honesty. I curled into her and I buried my face against her chest.

Why couldn't I make love to her like a normal person? Nope, not me. Now instead I was about to showcase all my craziness to her once again. I could feel a panic attack coming, rushing like a tidal wave, straight at me. The thing was, I realized, having a panic attack with her next to me, as sucky as that was, as much as I hated having her witness it, going through that with her was about a million times less sucky than having a panic attack alone.

~ CHAPTER 30 ~

AMANDA

It was happening again. Nick was having another panic attack. Rather than turning his back to me like last time, he pulled me closer and buried his face against my chest. His breath was hot and rapid, coming through the fabric of my shirt.

I dug my fingers into his thick hair, holding onto his head, wishing all over again I knew what to do. It was terrifying, feeling so hopeless, while I waited for him to get through it.

But he got through it. In only a few minutes, his breathing peaked and slowed. He calmed, but my heart kept on beating like mad to the tune of how heightened his rushed, shallow gulps of air had been.

I wanted to know how often this happened to him and what thoughts triggered it. I wanted to know how I could help. But that wasn't the conversation that followed. No words followed. Instead he pressed his mouth to mine—hot, demanding, and full of a sudden need. He kissed me hard. He kissed with a kind of desperation.

In the dark, he moved on top of me.

He pushed up the fabric of my shirt, peeling it off of my body. Next, he had his thumbs hooked on the edges of my underwear. He slid them down. I was completely naked in his bed. I couldn't see a thing, but I could feel him as he moved his hands and his lips to my skin. He pressed wet kisses from my navel up to my tightening nipples.

Oh God, I wanted him.

I'd stayed glued to the opposite side of his bed for over a week now—for this reason. Because the second he ran his hands over my skin, and moved his mouth to mine, I felt like I was buck-ass naked in the middle of a snowstorm—exposed and vulnerable—while Nick was the raging, relentless, icy wind against my skin.

I helped him tug off his shirt. I helped him work off his pants. I reached for him, feeling for his thick cock in the dark. I found his length; I felt all of him. He was hard. He was perfect. He practically had me drooling. I needed this man. I needed him inside me. Now. I needed to feel everything I already knew he knew how to give me.

He didn't hesitate.

He grabbed my body, turned me around, pulling my back to his chest. He pushed my legs wide open, running a hand over my center, across where I was wet and screaming for him. *Holy fuck!*

"Nick," I moaned, letting out a small cry, a small plea. Or maybe a small protest. I wasn't entirely sure.

"Lock your fingers behind my neck," he breathed against my ear. "Don't let go."

With shivers running all over me, I did as he instructed. I held onto his neck. He had his hands on my inner thighs. He touched me again in the center. He worked to move the head of his cock *right fucking there*. Then he guided himself inside.

I licked my lips, feeling all of him.

"Don't move your hands from my neck." His words were less of an instruction this time, more of a demand.

"I won't."

He pumped into me slowly. He circled his fingers over my clit. I held onto his neck like he'd asked. He was gentle. He was deliberately slow. When every ounce of me suddenly believed he was on the edge of being rough. A rougher version of Nick I'd never experienced before. I was here for whatever he needed right now.

"I want you to be mine," he whispered against my ear. He pressed his lips against me. He moved his body, sliding his cock inside me in slow strokes. "Mine, Amanda, only mine."

"I'm yours," I breathed. I said it without thinking. I knew right then that I was his. He had me. In every way, he already had me.

"You aren't. Not yet. But you will be."

It was a little hard to put sense to his words while he was inside me. But I realized he said those words because he still thought Finn was the baby's father. He didn't know that Finn and I were only friends, or that we'd never had a relationship at all. He didn't know it was only him I thought about, only his bed I wanted in each night after work, only him that I craved. He didn't know because before our few minutes of real conversation tonight, we'd barely spoken about much of anything.

He barely knew me. That was my fault.

His tempo changed. He started pounding into me harder, faster, rougher. He kept one of his hands in place against my clit, moving against me, fucking torturing me with his touch. A second like this and he had me coming.

I cried out, falling apart so easily for him, my body buzzing from the roots of my hair to the tips of my toes. I tingled all over. It was pure bliss coming at me at full force, full speed. I held on tighter to his neck. He didn't slow; he thrust harder. His hand moved relentlessly over my clit. One orgasm of mine melted into a second one.

He felt so damn amazing, but he kept going, kept thrusting his strength into me. He wasn't slowing to give me even a second to come down. He pushed me into a third orgasm before he finally came too. He released all his energy inside me, squeezing my thighs tight, pushing me open wider against where he was already so deep inside me. If I wasn't already pregnant, it would have felt like he was trying to put a baby inside me.

Fuck—was this him angry at me?

He was such a nice guy, but I realized... *yes, he was angry.* Knowing it, my heart raced. I think I'd just experienced my first ever 'angry fuck.' I'd enjoyed every bit of it, in a way, but he'd been controlling and a little forceful. Not the Nick I was used to. In the dark, I climbed away from him and felt for my shirt. I tugged it on once I found it.

I did the same with my underwear too.

"The baby's mine."

He was out of breath as he said these words. But he said them with such certainty that his voice hit me like a slap in the dark. *He knew? How did he know? Had he always known?* I climbed out of his bed, searching for my leggings and shoes.

"Answer me, Amanda. I'm right, aren't I? You lied to me. I'm falling hard for you. I hate it. I can't control it. Every girl I've ever loved ends up hurting me. All I can think is how you aren't going to be any different at all."

Wow. Just... wow.

"Yes. The baby is yours," I muttered. "Ding. Ding. You've got the correct answer."

I knew his anger was my fault. I should have told the truth from the start. I knew it was also my fault we barely knew each other; I'd been keeping my distance. But for him to jump to such conclusions... to say I wasn't any different than any ex of his. Then to add that to the way he'd just fucked me.

Like an object.

Like I meant so little to him.

I wasn't about to stick around a second longer.

"I gotta go, Nick. Thanks for the pie."

I left. I hadn't even found my shoes. And I wasn't sure if I'd ever come back. What an ass. When, up until this moment, I'd been thinking he was everything. But I was wrong. He could keep my damn shoes for all I cared.

~ CHAPTER 31 ~

AMANDA

The next few days at work were rough. I had to keep a straight face and go on like nothing had happened. The next day after the dinner, John Michaels came up to me, and commented on how he thought Nick seemed like a 'good guy.' I just nodded and agreed. Because John never, *ever* said stuff like that. He never went out of his way to make comments about anything. And for some reason, he chose to comment on Nick.

I couldn't correct my boss and tell him he was wrong. That Nick wasn't as perfect as he seemed. I also didn't want to admit I'd been wrong, *so completely wrong,* about him either. I guess he fooled us both. Maybe Chaz wasn't Nick's only alter ego. Maybe 'nice Nick' was complete bullshit too.

So I kept my mouth shut and a smile on my face. Even though I felt pretty broken inside. I also didn't mention a thing to Finn. I didn't need him angry.

Finn would flip out if he knew Nick had hurt me. He'd get in his car, drive to Nick's pretty rental house, and scream on his well-manicured lawn until he came outside.

I could picture it happening. It played out in my head like a bad movie.

I did nothing, said nothing. And I waited to see what Nick might do. Because this could be an easy out for him. He didn't have to be part of the baby's life if he didn't want to be. He could walk away, not look back, and that would be the end of that.

It took a week. But Nick did come to see me.

On a random Thursday, about an hour before we closed, Patrick walked into my station. "Your last appointment is here. It's Nick." He winked at me. "I'm going to take off early then since it's just you and Nick. Is that okay? I figure, we don't both have to be here, right?"

Nick moved into the doorway of my station, standing there, his blue eyes on me. He was so fucking handsome that my eyes dropped to the floor. My heart started screaming at me. If he moved closer, he might notice that my hands were now trembling.

"Yeah, that's fine, Patrick. Go ahead," I said to him, not wanting to seem awkward, not wanting to show weakness. My voice came out surprisingly calm even if calm was about the last thing I was feeling.

"Thanks, Amanda. Don't stay too late. You've been working a lot lately."

"I won't. And I'm fine." I sat down, busying myself with my tattooing equipment. As Patrick stepped away, Nick stepped closer, sitting down in my chair. Why did he have to smell so damn good *all the freaking time?* Because I swear, every time I was around him, his smell so intoxicating, it made me want him no matter the circumstances. And I hated him for that. Really, I did.

"Hi Amanda," he said to me. Plain. Simple. Easy going.

"Hi. Where the fuck are my sanitizing wipes?" I muttered to myself, searching, still avoiding his eyes.

"Right there." He pointed at them. They were two inches from my hands. "You look nice, by the way. You always look nice."

I took a deep breath. I stopped pretending to be busy. I stared straight at him. "What, Nick? What do you want? What are you doing here?"

"I have an appointment."

"Like a real appointment?"

"Yes. I called and set it up. You're hard to get an appointment with these days. It took me a week to get in. My tattoo isn't finished. It's just lines, and I can't live with *just lines* on my ass forever."

"Right." If I could have strangled him with my eyes, I would have. "Well, take off your pants then, I guess. Lay down."

He stared at me for a moment—*a long moment.* His face was so hard to read. Then he stood, tugging off his jeans, pulling off his underwear, letting both fall to the floor, before he lay stomach first on my chair. I swallowed hard, busying myself again with my tools, and pretended like seeing him half-naked had absolutely zero effect on me. But I did glance at his ass and at my previous work. Besides his original tattoo, the rest of the work I'd done on him was kind of a half-finished mess of lines.

I took a minute, finished getting my equipment ready. Then I touched him. I had to touch him to redraw everything all over again on his skin. I touched him, and it made me feel all jittery and shaky inside. It made my already-aching heart crack just a little more.

"You know, I'm not here for the tattoo," he said, his voice not quite as steady as before. "I really don't care about the tattoo. Or if I have random lines on my ass for the rest of my life. I came today because it's my baby inside you. You're showing by the way. Finally, I can tell a difference in your stomach. It's a small difference. But today I can tell a difference.

You're sexy just the same, by the way."

I couldn't do this.

I couldn't sit here, do his tattoo, and have a conversation like this. Not now. Not when I was feeling about ten different emotions, my heart was thudding against my ribs, and my stomach was in knots. "Nick, I can't finish this tattoo. I just can't. Maybe you should schedule an appointment with John or Finn instead."

~ CHAPTER 32 ~

NICK

Once again, I was using ink on my ass as an excuse to see this woman. I'd called the next day after our argument to make this appointment. I know I'd been a little rougher during sex than I should have been. That was inexcusable on my part. I shouldn't have acted on the emotions I was feeling post-panic attack. But I did. The primal fear, anxiety, rage—all of it bled straight into sex with her.

The sex had been damn good though. I think she'd partially agree with me on that. Because I *know* I'd gotten Amanda off several times. But when she grew upset afterwards, it made me realize she wasn't hanging around me for the hookup. For my cock, essentially. For the orgasms I could give her.

She wanted something more from me, and I loved her for that. I did. She'd gotten pretty deep under my skin. But she'd also lied about the baby all along. Why? Why would she lie so convincingly like that?

I waited a few days to see if she'd come sneak into my room again, so we could work this out, figure this out. But she never did. That was when I knew this appointment might be my only chance to speak with her.

"Maybe you should schedule an appointment with John or Finn instead," she told me, kind of shattering me a little bit more.

"I obviously don't want either of them finishing this tattoo." I sat up. Moving off her chair, grabbing my pants to pull on. I couldn't have such an important conversation without any pants. I got them back on and sat on the edge of the chair.

She peeled off her gloves, tossing them aside, putting her hands on her knees, shaking her head at me. "I'm not finishing it."

"I don't care about the tattoo."

"You should. It looks awful."

"I don't care. I'm sorry I wasn't as gentle as I should have been with you."

She narrowed her eyes at me, saying nothing.

"I'm sorry. I let too many emotions come out all at once. I try—" I took a deep breath, tugging my hands through my hair. I sure hoped Patrick was long gone at this point, so he wasn't hearing any of this. "I try to control everything I'm feeling all the time. My whole life is me working every second to maintain control. And I lost it for a moment with you. I'm sorry I let that happen. I'm showing you more of me now than I've ever shown anyone else. And all my control just slipped away that night. I'm sorry. It won't happen again."

"I feel like you 'hate fucked' me."

"What? That wasn't hate."

"Then what was it?"

"Not hate."

"Okay. Thanks for clarifying."

She had my stomach twisted. I gently put my hands on top of hers as they rested on her knees. "Hey," I muttered. I needed her to look at me. Because she wasn't, and I couldn't talk to her without having her eyes on me. At my touch, her brown eyes rose to mine. "I promise that wasn't hate. I would never 'hate fuck' you." I could barely repeat the words. The idea that she believed me capable of that and had been believing all that this past week made me feel sick. "Can I show you what that was?"

She gave a small shrug. "Whatever. Sure."

I removed my hands from her hands. "Not hate," I muttered again. I touched her arms. My fingertips traced slowly upward until they reached her shoulders. I curved over them then moved my touch up her neck. I wasn't in a hurry. I wasn't doing this to turn her on. I just wanted to show her what she meant to me, how much I savored every time and place I got to touch her. Cupping her face, I ran my thumbs along her jaw. "So far from hate."

I kissed her.

All soft and slow and controlled.

Or was I in control? I could feel my heart was speeding away from me. The fear of losing her—I felt it buzzing on my skin. She could break me, I realized. So easily. If this was our last kiss, it would cripple me. At some point I'd given her my heart, without even realizing how or when, and now she had me at her mercy.

She pulled back first, and I moved away.

Blood was thumping in my ears. My whole world hung on how she would respond to that kiss. Did she feel even a fraction of what I felt? Her eyes weren't on mine.

"I'd really love if you came over to sleep in my bed again," I said to her. "Just sleep. You can have your side. I'll have mine."

"Or... you could come sneak into my house. Into my bed. There's a door in the back. I'll leave a key under the mat." She shrugged. Fuck, she was stubborn. And terrified to show me too much—a thought that suddenly dawned on me.

"I'll come later tonight."

"Do whatever you want. It's not like I'm going to wait up for you."

"I'll come. Same time you always came to my room. Bye Amanda, see you in a couple hours." I got up to leave but paused. "I am going to wait in my car in the parking lot first and make sure I see you get to your car safely. Since it's just you closing up alone now. So, think nothing of that." I started to go again but paused for a second time. "Even if the baby were Finn's, I'd still have come here tonight just the same. Even if there were no baby, just the same. But I am glad it's mine."

I left her then.

She'd given me permission to come over later. The last thing I wanted to do was say too much and have her change her mind. But I'd show up and I'd keep showing up however many times it took for her to finally let her guard down.

~ CHAPTER 33 ~

AMANDA

I heard a bang in the kitchen. It was Nick. He was here. Again. He'd been coming over nightly for the past week, and every time he came into the house, always around midnight, he'd stub his toe or trip over something. I smiled to myself because tonight was no different.

He made it to the bedroom. I always pretended to be asleep at this point. He crawled into bed, sticking to the right side.

I stuck to the left.

Now that he was here, I closed my eyes. He'd be gone when I woke up in the morning. He always was. We were good at this—the sleeping in the same bed with zero interaction thing. I often wondered what he was getting out of it. Why he kept showing up. But he kept showing without fail. Once, he even left me take-out breakfast in my fridge. I hated that he'd seen my tiny, rundown house, including my 1980's refrigerator now too, but I guess it wasn't deterring him from coming each night.

After so many days of not talking to each other, again, really for no reason at all, tonight he spoke. "I got my job back. Finally," he said to the dark. "Or a job at least."

I guess he knew I was awake.

Or maybe he was testing to see if I'd answer.

"You weren't working?" I whispered.

"I quit when I planned to leave. Then I went back for my job and they'd filled my position. Which was upsetting, but I couldn't do much about it. My old boss called today. The North Carolina Aquatic Preservation Society received some grant money, enough to hire another marine biologist, and they asked me to come back. It's temporary. It's not as much money as I was making before. It's good for as long as the grant money lasts. Which will be about two years."

I turned against the sheets, facing his direction, facing his voice. "So no matter what, you'll be here for the next two years?"

"Yes."

"And then after that?"

"I'll figure something else out. I'm not going to leave the city where my kid lives. Not for any job. There's an aquarium on Roanoke Island. I'll keep checking for positions there. They have a sea turtle rehabilitation center there as well."

Him and his sea turtles.

I loved how passionate he seemed to be about them. I also loved the way he said he wouldn't leave his kid. It made my chest feel all warm and slippery.

"What do you do every day? If you aren't working, I mean." I wondered because he always left here before the sun came up. Even when I stayed in his bed, I never left so early. Was he in that much of a hurry to get away each day? Plus, who was paying the bills on his rental house? His parents, I assumed.

"I've started volunteering with the NEST team. I do it every morning now."

"What's that?" I asked.

"Just a team of ATV riders who go out to the beaches each morning looking for sea turtle nests. There's sixty miles of beach to cover every morning. Then if we find a nest we call the nesting response team. They mark off the nest for protection, identify which type of sea turtle's nest it is, and take one egg for DNA testing. I used to be part of that team. So I stick around and help the response team sometimes. But yeah, that's what I'm always doing. Where I go in the mornings."

"Oh." It sounded like he was working his ass off each day. "And when do the nests hatch? I'll admit, I've lived at the Outer Banks my whole life and don't know much about sea turtles at all."

"They'll hatch about fifty to ninety days later. Depends on the species. There's a night team for when they hatch. Mostly local volunteers for that. I volunteer with the night team too. So if I'm ever missing from your bed at night, that's where I am."

"Are you going tomorrow? With the ATV team?"

"Yes."

"Can I go?"

"What? Really? You want to go ride an ATV with me?"

Hell yes. At sunrise. On the beach. With him. I could do that. I would love to do that. "Sure."

"Okay. Tomorrow, then. Goodnight, Amanda."

He cut me off when it felt like we were vibing so well. But instead of being upset, I snuggled my pillow a little tighter, happy for even that small amount of conversation with him. "Goodnight, Nick," I breathed, smiling.

I couldn't stop smiling.

And it took me forever to fall asleep.

~ CHAPTER 34 ~

NICK

What was I thinking? Obviously, I wasn't thinking. I shouldn't have agreed to bring Amanda. I should have thought this through. Now that she was here, her arms around my waist, with pink on the ocean's horizon, I had to stop the ATV.

"It's too bumpy." I cut the ignition and pocketed its key. "I thought if I went slow enough it wouldn't be as bumpy. But I can't. I can't risk this. You shouldn't be riding an ATV while pregnant. It doesn't feel safe."

What the hell was I thinking? I'd only driven about twenty feet, but every bump, even the smallest of them, was making me feel sick to my stomach with worry and fear. What if one of these bumps hurt our baby? At this point, if something happened to our baby, I don't know how I'd survive it. I was already incredibly invested in this. "I have to get up," I said to her. "Your arms around my waist feel so damn nice. But I have to get up." I pulled out of her grip, and I climbed off the ATV. Way too dramatically, I realized, but so much of that familiar acidic feeling was building inside my veins.

I stood in the cool sand, my chest rising and falling with each colossal breath I took, and I stared at the ocean.

She got off the ATV, and I felt her come stand beside me. "You okay?"

"That was too much anxiety, too soon in the day. I can't... we can't."

"Okay," she said softly, calmly, not at all upset with me. "We don't have to. Honestly, looking for turtle nests, that wasn't why I wanted to come so much. I just—" She breathed out. "I just wanted another chance to do something with you. Outside of the bedroom."

She touched my arm—a brush of her fingers against my skin.

I thought about Emma for a small second. About how she never said stuff like this, stuff that made me feel, honestly, so goddamned special.

The sun was making its break over the horizon, and I dropped to the sand. I tugged her hand. I pulled her body down into my lap. Then I wrapped my arms around her. Only seeing her at night meant I wasn't actually seeing her at all. In the last week, her body had changed, and in the daylight today I could see that. Her stomach had grown a little bigger to the point that it was no longer so easy for her the hide the evidence of what was happening inside her.

She fit so perfectly against me. I had never been this lost in love with anyone before. It was frightening, scary, exciting, and even a little bit maddening.

I fought every single day not to touch her, when all I wanted to do was touch her. I needed to call one of the other ATV riders to cover my miles, but that could wait just a few more minutes.

I held her over her stomach. So many feelings were flooding through me. I tried to control everything I felt—

All. The. Fucking. Time.

Right now I just kind of let them rush through me. It surprised me when a panic attack didn't follow. It was just her and me, the ocean, the salty breeze, and the morning sun on our skin.

"There's something amazing here," I told her, swallowing hard. My throat felt thick. "Something unexpected and crippling, but so fucking amazing. You induce anxiety, in the best way. I've never had that before. Good anxiety. I didn't know it existed. I feel like... *holy fuck,* is what I feel with you." I buried my face against her shoulder.

She wasn't saying anything in response. But she tightened her hands over my grip around her middle. She moved a little against me, almost like she was trying to get closer.

"Okay," I said after a few minutes. "I've got to call Bobby. He can get someone else to cover my miles today. Let's go."

By now the sun had risen enough in the sky that the air was warming. The best parts of the sunrise had passed. She stood. I stood. We walked off the beach, hand-in-hand this time. And I swear to God, something had shifted between us.

We'd always had a great connection. But now, I don't know what had happened exactly, it was magnified by ten. Every look between us gave me little jolts of electricity. Every small touch made my skin tingle.

Shit.

I was so done. I was so in love.

I couldn't do much to contain the smile she kept bringing to my lips.

~ CHAPTER 35 ~

AMANDA

Maybe sitting and watching a sunrise with this man hadn't been my best idea. Because now I was feeling dizzy, literally dizzy in his presence. He was fogging my brain, and I couldn't decide if this was a good thing.

We'd left the beach and now he was speaking on the phone to someone named Bobby. I briefly wondered if it was the same Bobby I knew, my dad's old friend. But I'd known Bobby my whole life, and I think I would have known if he was out riding ATVs every morning looking for turtles.

"No one is at the shop right now," I said to him once he was off the phone. "And they won't be for a few hours. Want to go and I could work on your tattoo today?"

"Yeah. We could do that."

His eyes were on the road. Despite agreeing, I couldn't tell if he was super thrilled by this idea. Sometimes he was easy to read. Sometimes he wasn't. And I didn't have a clue what was on his mind now.

"We don't have to," I added.

"I would like to."

What if all of this was too much too soon? "We could keep avoiding each other except at night. I didn't mean to suddenly switch up our good thing today."

Or maybe I *had* meant to do exactly that, I realized. I think I was finally ready to really dig into this thing I felt with Nick. But was he?

"No, I'd like to go," he repeated.

"You sure?"

"I'm sure."

He took a turn and instead of heading in the direction of my home, he headed to the place where everything started for us. *Kill Devil Ink.*

I had a key. I think all of us except Patrick had a key. After we were out of the car, I unlocked the front door to the shop and Nick followed me inside. The bell on the door chimed loudly against the quiet, still morning. The sun coming in the front windows showed off little particles of dust floating the air. It really reminded me of that morning John caught us naked. But I wasn't doing anything I shouldn't be doing today. And, looking back on it now, I was no longer that embarrassed about that morning he found us.

We went back to my station.

"Alright," I said to him. "I guess… take off your pants."

I couldn't help but smile a little at my words.

"Sure," he said quietly. But he wasn't shy at the way he dropped his pants, that was for damn certain. He pulled them down and climbed onto his stomach in my chair. I didn't look. I pretended like I was too busy getting my tools ready. For any other customer who was getting ink done on their ass, I wouldn't have been so casual. I would have stepped away and given them their privacy. I would have given them something to cover up with. I figured, with him and I, what did it matter?

But I hoped I wasn't making him feel uncomfortable. "Nick," I said to him. He was on his stomach and his face was resting on his forearms. The last time he was here we'd gotten into a huge fight. I hadn't apologized yet for my part in that fight. But I needed to. "I'm sorry I lied about our baby. I'm sorry I said it was Finn's."

I grabbed an alcohol wipe, opened the paper, and started prepping his skin for more ink.

"I guess I've never had anyone like you interested in me before. You're smarter than any guy I've ever dated. Better looking. Better in bed. Better at making me come, obviously. And I am constantly questioning why you're interested in me. So when I said it was Finn's, I think I did it because I wanted to see how you'd react. To see if you could still be interested in me. Because, I knew a good guy like you—I knew you'd stick around for your baby. But I wanted to know first if you'd stick around for just me."

"Wow," he muttered.

It was all he said.

My heart was pounding so hard. My hands were feeling tingly. But I ignored everything I felt, took the red pen, and started drawing on his skin. I didn't get out my phone to look at my past designs. I had a new idea and decided to try it instead.

"I'm better in bed than anyone you've been with?" he muttered. I could hear the humor in his voice and the curiosity. "Better at making you come?"

He was such a guy. Of course he would fixate on that. "Yes." I shook my head. "Don't let it go to your head."

"Better than Finn?"

"I've never been with Finn."

"Not at all?"

"No. We kissed once but it was awkward as hell." I made a face as I was drawing on him. "Super awkward. And then we became friends."

"Wow, I like Finn so much better now."

I laughed out loud.

Then I continued drawing. But I noticed Nick smiling, a little hint of a cocky grin on his lips. He had a cocky, confident side to his personality, one I'll admit I kind of adored, and I guess I didn't mind feeding that confidence. He was so damn sexy with that confidence. I bit down on my lip. I needed to focus on my work instead of on his beautiful face, on his beautiful ass.

After a few minutes, I finished with the red pen.

"You want to see my design? I changed it a little."

It was grittier now, more open lines, more jagged edges. I didn't hold back; I just went for what I felt. It was raw, a whole new level to my design style.

I loved it.

"Surprise me at the end."

"You're crazy."

"No, I trust you as an artist."

I worked for the next four hours. We stayed even after John arrived to open the shop for the day. Today was my day off. But I felt good, my morning sickness wasn't bothering me much today, and so I kept working. I worked past noon until the piece was completely finished.

Nick's skin was angry and bright red.

It was a lot of work for one day.

My heart was flip-flopping all over the place when I handed him the mirror to see his own ass. I waited on his comments. He smiled—this big smile that told me he loved it. His blue eyes met mine, and I knew I was crazy about him.

I'd been afraid to tell him the baby was his for this very reason. Because now he had my heart in the palm of his hand. If he squeezed, even a little bit, he could crush it to pieces. No one had ever held that kind of power over me. I think I knew all along, that this guy was going to be like that for me. I knew I needed to keep him at arm's length for as long as I could for my own safety. I hadn't been successful at that. Because, as much as I tried to tell myself I wasn't, I think I was in love with him now. And I'd never been more terrified of anything in my whole life.

~ CHAPTER 36 ~

NICK

I didn't know I could like something so much. Amanda showed me the fresh ink she'd spent half the day putting on my ass, using a mirror she'd used with me before, and it was better than I could have expected. It was amazing. She was so damn talented. I hoped she realized that. How could she not realize it? The evidence of it was literally on my skin.

I glanced at her face. Her cheeks were flushed. "Do you like it?"

She radiated with a vulnerability as she asked me this. What I thought clearly meant a lot to her. "It's perfect. Can you fix me up now, doc? I'd really like to take you out to lunch now. I mean… if you're up for it. I've been listening to your stomach growl for the last thirty minutes."

"Sorry about that."

"Don't apologize for being hungry. But let's get out of here so we can get lunch."

She gave me a small nod.

I wanted to grab her, kiss her, hug her. I didn't. At this point, I didn't know what was okay between us. Or where we stood exactly. But the way she was being shy and quiet around me told me that wherever we were, it was a good place. I figured for now it was better to fight any impulse that ran through me, and just stick to doing things I knew were safe. Lunch—that seemed safe.

She applied some sort of petroleum jelly to my ink before bandaging me up. Just the way she took care of me told me so much about her personality. Her soft touches and her attention to detail (*for my ass!*) reflected those qualities I already knew I loved about her. I could picture her being just as gentle with our baby once it came.

"How many weeks are you?" I asked. I still didn't know for sure where she was in her pregnancy and suddenly, I had a million questions. I couldn't keep riding backseat to this anymore. I wanted upfront, in the passenger seat. I wanted to be a bigger part. I wanted her to confide in me and tell me everything that was happening.

"Seventeen weeks. It's the size of a pear this week."

"A pear, already? That's huge. You haven't found out the sex yet, right?"

"No."

"Oh good." I tugged my underwear and pants up over the bandage, over *myself.* I'd had my pants down around her like this, all casual, so many times now that it wasn't a big deal anymore. "If it's okay with you, I'd really like to go with you to that appointment."

"You can come."

"Thanks," I breathed.

We were suddenly only inches apart. Maybe it had something to do with the excitement I felt in this moment over our baby, but I felt this connection with her that was almost electric. The air around us was buzzing. My heart raced and my fingertips tingled. They were tingling with the need to touch her skin—touch more than her skin. The need was practically vibrating through me. It was a damn good feeling. More of that good kind of anxiety.

"Yo. Amanda." It was Finn, completely interrupting, barging into Amanda's station. I took a breath and a step away from Amanda, closing my eyes for a small second, composing myself.

"And Nick," Finn added. "John said you were both here. That's good. I need to talk to you." I thought for a second, he meant talk to Amanda. But he crossed his arms over his large chest and was staring straight at me.

"What do you want?"

"Lou. I need to know more about your roommate, Lou."

What the fuck!

He shouldn't know Lou's name. Why would he know her name? He had no reason to know it. Unless Lou had been out of the house, doing stuff, talking to people. Which was absurd with her agoraphobia. Maybe Amanda had been talking about Lou with Finn—which seemed more likely than her being out of the house. But why would Amanda have any reason to talk about Lou with him?

"What do you want to know about Lou?" I asked as casually as I possibly could.

"Anything at this point."

I ran my hands through my hair. He sounded like a man 'interested' in a woman. Interested in fucking her. I knew relatively little about Finn. But I knew enough to know he had absolutely zero business being interested in a girl like Lou. To my knowledge, Lou had never even kissed a boy in her life. Finn was the type of guy who probably went around kissing—*kissing and fucking*—his way through as many women as he possibly could. Lou, from a distance, probably seemed all mysterious and beautiful to him. Fresh meat. I could see a guy like him trying to prey on all her vulnerabilities.

"Stay the fuck away from Lou," I said as calmly as possible. "I need to go. How much do I owe you for the ink, Amanda?"

"Nothing," she muttered. "This time it's on me."

"No. I'm not going to *not* pay you. But we'll sort it out another day. I'm sorry, I've got to take a raincheck on lunch."

"That's fine."

I was done here. Honestly, I didn't like the way Amanda wasn't interjecting and asking Finn a million questions, the same million questions I wanted to demand of him. It meant that maybe she had spoken about Lou with him before. The few things I'd told her about Lou had been in confidence. She shouldn't have shared anything she knew with Finn. I needed to get home and find out from her what this was all about.

"I'll see you in bed later tonight," I said to Amanda, not entirely sure I would.

Then I left.

I left so fast I felt the world spin.

Back at the house, things were calm. Between staying every night at Amanda's and all my recent job hunting and volunteering, I hadn't seen much of Lou lately. I shopped for her groceries. I checked in on her. But mostly, I assumed she was fine on her own—inside. Maybe she wasn't. Maybe a guy like Finn had been coming around and she needed me to get him to back the fuck off.

I took the deck steps two at a time, pushing open the front door in a rush. Lou was standing in the kitchen, eating cereal from a bowl. I opened the door so fast I startled her, and she dropped the bowl to the floor. Milk and Fruit Loops went everywhere.

"Nick!" she screeched.

"What's going on with Finn?" I demanded.

"Who? Who's Finn?"

I could hear it. The lie in her voice. She knew who Finn was. She definitely did. We'd only had about fifty conversations about him and Amanda. Speculations over him being the father to my child or not. Since I found out Finn wasn't the father, we'd stopped talking about him altogether. But I knew she hadn't forgotten his name in the short time since that discovery.

Right that moment, someone knocked on my front door.

For a split second, I thought it might have been Amanda following after me, coming to explain. It wasn't her. The intruder announced themselves.

"Knock. Knock," said a familiar voice. "Nick, honey. Lou? It's Mom."

My mom, out of nowhere, let herself right into my house. *What the hell was she doing here all the way from Maine?* But I wasn't too surprised to see my mom suddenly standing in my house. She'd always come, visit me by surprise like this when I was in college.

"Mom?"

"Mrs. Jasmine?" Lou asked.

"Hi, kids! Surprise. I brought some moon pies." She held up what looked like a plastic cupcake container full of her favorite kind of cookie/pie, the only one she loved making and bringing as a gift. Had she driven? Had she flown? She could have called, but that wasn't her style. "Samantha's with me." Samantha was Mick's thirteen-year-old stepdaughter. "She's bringing in more stuff from the car." Mom came over and wrapped her strong arms around my shoulders, squeezing me like we hadn't seen each other in a couple years.

"Perfect timing, Mom," I said against her perfectly styled blonde hair. "Perfect timing. As usual. But it's good to see you."

She let me go. She had tears in her eyes. That was just Mom's way. She was always overwhelmed with joy whenever she first saw me. She gave Lou a hug next, and I watched Lou squirm and wiggle in agony as she did it.

Well, this was going to be loads of fucking fun. I had Lou's situation to figure out. I had everything with Amanda I needed to keep pursuing. Now I had Mom staying in my house. I hadn't mentioned to my parents I had a new girlfriend. If that's what Amanda was. I hadn't mentioned I had a baby on the way. Those were things that weren't so easy to bring up in conversation. But since Mom was here… I guess, no time like the present.

"Guess what," I said to her. "I have a girlfriend."

"Guess what," Lou echoed. "I think I might have a boyfriend."

Fuck. I buried my face in my hands.

"I can't wait to meet them both!" Mom squealed. These were like magic words to a mother. "Let's have them both over for dinner tonight."

"Hell. No."

"Please, Nick," Mom said. "That sounds wonderful."

"No. Just no. Lou doesn't have a boyfriend."

"How do you know I don't?" Lou interjected.

I had to step away. Between the two of them, I was going to get pushed over the edge, bring on too much stress that might lead to my next panic attack.

~ CHAPTER 37 ~

AMANDA

Nick was gone. He'd left in such a hurry too. I could tell Finn merely *mentioning* Lou's name had upset him. It upset him more than maybe it should have. Which might have been a little concerning, but I honestly knew so little about Lou that it was impossible to judge Nick's reaction—if it was an overreaction or a justified reaction, I didn't know. It bugged me that I didn't know.

"What the hell?" I yelled at Finn once Nick was long gone. I slapped Finn's big, tattooed, muscular arm. "Seriously? What was that about?"

"What do you know about Lou?"

"What do *you* know about her?" I threw back at him.

The only thing I knew about Lou was that she lived with Nick and that she had agoraphobia. Oh, and not to mention, she was insanely fucking beautiful. I'd only seen her the one time, in this shop, when she'd walked in with him and had a hoodie over her long blonde hair. Finn saw her that day, too. I wondered now about Nick's relationship with her. He hadn't mentioned her since that very first night I went over to his house, when he said she had agoraphobia and that she was like a sister to him. I'd believed him completely, and that was that. So I'd never had reason to question him until now.

Finn let out a big breath. "She's different. She's funny about space and people. She's fucking smart, like book smart, but also completely clueless about the littlest things. Like maybe she grew up with the Amish or something."

"Wait. Wait. Go back. But *how* do you know her, Finn? Like *why do you know her at all?*" I questioned him slowly. I moved across the front lobby and sat down on one of John's precious brown leather couches. I motioned for Finn to follow. The morning was catching up with me. I'd pushed myself to complete Nick's tattoo, pushed myself maybe a little too hard, when that sort of work was starting to become harder and harder for me lately.

My back was sore. My arms were sore.

Finn moved over to the couches with me. There was a customer waiting, possibly on John, possibly on Finn, and she sat on the opposite couch. I really didn't care if she heard any of this. "How do you know her?" I repeated.

"I went over to Nick's rental house. I did a little detective work to get his address. Because earlier at work that day you seemed off. I think I'd asked you that morning if everything was good. You said everything was fine like ten times. Which, after your dad died, you used to always say *'fine, everything is fine,'* all the fucking time. And I don't think anything was fine for you after he died. So I went over to Nick's house later that night after I'd stewed on it all day. I knocked on his door. Felt like an idiot because your car wasn't even in his driveway. But there were lights on, and then I figured since I'd gone all the way over to his house that I might as well confront him. Hell. Fuck." Finn pushed his fingers through the strands of his hair. "Maybe even tell that asshole I wasn't the baby's father. Because him believing that I was, was really starting to fucking eat me up."

"Crap," I whispered. "Finn, I'm sorry I—"

"No, it's whatever. Lou tells me he knows now. That you told him like days back, so that's good. Good for you guys. Anyway, so I knock on the door. It's her voice on the other side. Lou and I talked through the door for a while. She said he was staying at your place instead of you at his. Long story short, I've been going there and talking to that girl through her damn door every single night since."

I stared at him, at the little wrinkle between his eyebrows. "The only thing I know about her is that she has agoraphobia," I told him. I said it because if Finn was starting to fall for this girl, which it seemed like maybe he was, then he deserved to know that much.

"Yeah, no shit."

"Oh. I guess you know more about her than me."

"I guess." He sat back on the leather, breathing in deeply. "I fucked up earlier though with Nick; I'll admit that. I guess, when I said Lou's name to him, I wasn't necessarily after information. I can get information from the source. I guess, I just wanted Nick to know I knew her. I wanted you both to know something was happening between us. Maybe if you all knew, it would feel more real. Something like that. I don't know. I approached the situation all wrong though. I know I did."

I'd never seen this side to Finn. He seemed concerned but also calm. Very levelheaded and calm. He joked, he laughed, he talked a lot. But talking about the women he dated... he usually didn't do much of that.

"Okay." I stood up. "So should we go over there? Go to Nick's house. See them both."

"No. Hell, no. That's not how Lou and I work. Just, you keep doing your thing with Nick. I'll keep doing my thing with Lou. We'll leave it at that for now. We don't have to all be friends, go on double dates, and shit."

Finn stood. He moved past me.

"Okay," I muttered to myself.

I still didn't like the way Nick had left the shop earlier. We'd been having such a good day, and the way it had abruptly ended made my stomach feel a little nauseated. But I didn't have much time to think on those feelings because at that second the phone to the shop rang. Finn had just disappeared down the hall, and I didn't know where Patrick was today. So I had no choice, I grabbed the phone to answer it.

"Thanks for calling *Kill Devil Ink.* This is Amanda. What can I help you with?"

"This is Nick."

"Oh," I whispered, clutching the big plastic phone in my hand. "I um... hi."

"Hey, sorry about earlier. I'm glad you're still there. I'm glad I caught you. I don't have your phone number. I don't think you have mine either. We need to fix that. So, Lou's in some kind of denial and thinks Finn is her boyfriend. But that's not why I called. Want to still meet for lunch? I'm not feeling well enough to go out for it though. I thought maybe we could meet at your house. We could have lunch there?"

My heart was pounding. Nick's voice against my ear had the organ beating around like a possessed drum inside my chest. He'd only ever seen the inside of my house when it was the middle of the night. What would he think if he saw it for what it really was in the light of day? We'd also never hung out like this so casually.

But I wanted it.

I needed it, even.

"Sure. Meet me there in thirty minutes. Does that work?"

"Perfect. I'll bring the food. Bye, Amanda."

"Bye, Nick."

I hung up the phone. Then I left. The girl, the lone customer, was still sitting on the couch and she looked at me as I left, all annoyed, but I hardly cared about her. I hardly cared about much right this moment except meeting Nick at my house.

~ CHAPTER 38 ~

NICK

Amanda's house was small and dated. I'd only ever seen it in the pitch black of the night, meaning I'd basically never seen it. But today I saw the inside in full light.

The furniture she owned was stuffed into the house a little awkwardly, sort of like trying to pack an extra crayon into the crayon box. There were many framed pictures on the wall, a lot of them nautical. Then there was Amanda. Her pink hair was a contrast to the neutral colors of her home. But even if the home was small, there was something I loved about her place. It had a cozy, comfortable, homey feel, and something, it was hard to put my finger on, screamed her name.

I let myself in the same way I always did at night. And I found her sitting cross-legged on her couch with a sketch pad in her lap. She set it aside when she saw me. This version of her inside her home was one I wasn't familiar with. Not yet, at least.

"How's your ass?" she said to me.

"On fire, actually, thanks." On her coffee table, made of solid stained-gray oak, I set down the takeout bag I'd brought with me. It was so far past lunch time by this point, and I hoped she'd already eaten a little something by now.

"You still have on the bandaging, right?"

"I haven't touched it."

"Tonight you can take it off. Then wash it the way I told you before. You have the mild, fragrance free kind of soap, right? Then—"

"Amanda," I cut her off. "I know."

"It's just—"

"I know. You've explained this a couple times now. Not my first tattoo anymore."

"Okay." She gave me a small, shy smile. "Hi."

"Hi," I returned.

Fuck, one word from her and warmth flooded my body. She had that effect on me.

"What'd you get?" She reached to peek inside the takeout bag. I sat down carefully on her solid-wood coffee table. My ass really was on fire. Sitting wasn't comfortable.

"I went to the key lime pie place." I shrugged, taking her in some more. She was in a white tank top, her pink hair hit the ink on her shoulders, and her little bit of stomach showing was cute as hell.

"You got me key lime pie?"

"I did."

I was really enjoying this moment. It was calm in her house. Being around her—it was like a warm summer day back home in Maine, the breeze blowing past the curtains, the sunshine streaming in. That was what her home felt like—seeing her sitting on her couch, pregnant and all—it felt like home. Jesus, and it was getting to me.

She paused when she caught me staring at her. She stood. Looking down at me, she took my hand. "Come on," she muttered. "Come with me."

I didn't know what she wanted but I stood with her. I followed her as she led me through her house, deeper down the narrow, dimly lit hallway, toward her bedroom. I noticed a second bedroom I hadn't before. I think that meant in total her place had only the two bedrooms.

Inside her room, she softly closed her door. It clicked shut. Then she came to me, she rested her palms on my chest, and she stared up at me.

Fuck.

I couldn't help the smile that grew naturally on my lips. Damn. I didn't stand a chance. I understood now why she'd dragged me back to her bedroom. What she wanted. My heart was beating like a maniac in my chest because of it. Her room smelled like her. Warm. Sweet. Maddening. It had been way too many nights sleeping in her bed, sleeping so close to her, never touching her.

But I felt the walls crumbling away.

I moved my hands to her neck. Her skin felt so damn good, so soft under my fingertips. I made a noise deep in my throat, pushing my forehead to hers. "You have me," I said to her softly. My voice came out raw, a little gritty. "I don't know if you know that. Fuck, you probably do already know that. But I'm yours."

Through her lashes, her brown eyes came to meet mine. "Don't say stuff like that unless you mean it."

"I mean it." I don't know what I'd ever done that would give her the impression I didn't mean it. Because I'd never meant anything more in my life.

I moved my lips to hers. I wanted to show her just how much I meant it. I kissed her. I kissed her with all the emotions I felt pumping through my veins. Guiding her with my body, I moved her toward the bed.

All my control—it melted away.

~ CHAPTER 39 ~

AMANDA

Nick's hands moved in slow motion over my skin. No one had ever touched me so softly, so carefully, so unrushed. There was an entirely different air between us, reflected in the tempo he set. "Oh God, Nick," I breathed when he pushed his way carefully inside me. It had been too many days since we last slept together, and my body screamed for what I knew he could give me.

He pulled back out. All the way out. Then he guided himself back in, repeating the slow, wonderful torture. "Nick." I moved to rest my arms above my head. "Dammit, Nick."

He kept with his slow way.

Moving, gliding, in and out.

Careful. Controlled.

And it felt good as hell.

But something about it terrified me. Terrified me to my core. "Harder," I whispered. "Harder, please."

I knew I was all over the map. I knew I told him last time he'd been too rough. Now I wanted to tell him he was being too soft. Not because I wasn't enjoying it. But because this was fucking stirring up way too many emotions inside me.

He moved his hands to my neck. They were warm against my skin. He bent closer, his mouth to my ear, and he whispered, "I don't ever want to give you the impression that we're *hate-fucking* again. Or whatever you called it."

I had tears in my eyes.

"Because hate isn't what I'm feeling with you, Amanda. Not even close."

"What are you feeling?" I whispered.

He stopped moving. He froze in place on top of me.

I shouldn't have asked.

I shouldn't have asked.

I shouldn't have asked.

"Love."

His eyes met mine. He paused for a moment, then finished his thought.

"I'm in love with you, Amanda."

He took a breath and rolled off me, collapsing on the bed beside me for a brief moment. But he didn't rest for long. I knew I needed to say something, but I was finding it impossible to do much more than breathe.

"I have to get this bandage off my ass. Its bugging the hell out of me. Do you mind if I use your shower?"

"Sure." I choked out the word.

He was up, out of bed, and moving toward the bathroom connected to my room. He disappeared inside. I heard the sound of the shower starting. I sat up in bed, burying my face in my hands. *What was wrong with me? Could I have handled that any worse?*

I loved him too. My chest felt tight and warm, and it was screaming at me because I loved him so much.

I got out of bed and marched into the bathroom after him. He was in my shower. This gorgeously fit, sexy-as-hell man was in my shower, his dark hair visible above the curtain line. I pulled back the shower curtain on him. He looked so freaking out of place in there. The tile needed updating. My array of shampoo bottles, the cheapest brand they sell at Walmart, cluttered up the small area. The water came out as more of a drip than actual pressure on him because I couldn't afford the plumbing that needed attention. He had my bar soap, all sudsy on his skin, and his hand moved in circular motions on his ass just like I'd told him to do earlier today when I gave my spiel on tattoo care.

"Nick!" I yelled at him. "What the fuck, Nick!"

"What?"

"I'm in love with you, too."

"Well, that's a relief. Get in the shower."

"No. You're too fucking good looking. Look at you in there." I had my eyes on his beautiful body. "I mean, come on. What are you doing with me? Is it just the baby?"

"You know it's not just the baby. Get in the shower."

"No. I didn't go to college. I barely graduated high school. And you should have seen my dad when I graduated, he was so proud of me for doing just that. This house—it was my dad's house. The only reason I own this rundown thing is because he died and left it to me. You and Emma—I understand that. She's pretty and perfect and sweet. You guys… I don't understand why you two didn't work, because trust me, Caleb Mills has nothing on you. So the guy can sing—big fucking deal. I'm going to slap that girl upside her pretty head the next time I see her. Because not even

Rockstar Caleb Mills is on your level."

"Get in the shower."

"No. I'm not finished. I'm afraid I won't be a great mom. I'm alone. I don't know if you've noticed that. But I'm not good at making friends. My only real friend is Finn, probably because Finn could be friends with a rock. I'm just kind of a loner. That never concerned me before, but it concerns me now. Who am I going to ask for advice on baby stuff?"

"Me. It'll be me."

This was it. This was why I was so terrified. I was afraid this sexy, handsome, heart-pounder, panty-dropper of a man would eventually come to his senses and ditch me. Ditch me and our baby. Then I'd be more alone than ever. I could handle being alone when it was only me to worry about. But with a baby? How was I going to care for a baby all on my own?

Nick's interest in me didn't made sense. I think that was why I accused him of 'hate-fucking' me last week. Because even his out-of-control, wild passionate sex didn't make sense. I'd never inspired that kind of love-making in any guy I'd been with before. Maybe the ink on my skin gave the impression that I was unique and cool, wild and fun. But underneath, inside, I had always felt exceptionally average.

In bed. In life. In love.

Average. So unexcitingly average.

He hit the nozzle for the shower, turning it off. "I'm going to take care of you. You and our little pear. Why do you think I've been spending so much time volunteering? Because I needed to get my job back. I needed to have that income... for you, for our baby. I like sea turtles, Amanda, but not *that* fucking much." He moved a little closer, his hand grabbing the shower curtain. "I'm sorry about your dad. I can tell you really loved him and you miss him. I'll be your person. I promise I'll be your person. I suck ass at making friends too. We can be loners together. And the real truth is, Emma Winchester isn't on your fucking level. Not even close."

I stared up at his blue eyes, his dark lashes wet from the water. It was quiet in the bathroom. My heart pounded in my chest. He had me at one word—*pear*. He called our baby a pear, and nothing had ever hit me harder.

"Get in the shower." He repeated softly.

I listened this time.

I stepped in carefully, and the moment I did, Nick wrapped his arms around my shoulders. He pressed his wet body in against mine. I closed my eyes. He felt like heaven. If heaven were a person, a feeling—it would be Nick.

~ CHAPTER 40 ~

NICK

Before I knew it, it was morning, the following day. Amanda—beautiful, naked, asleep—lay next to me, snuggled under the covers. I didn't want to wake her. I didn't want to move. But I needed to go before I was late again for volunteering with the ATV riders. My mind kept replaying moments from our night together.

The shower.

Fuck me, that shower. After our conversation, we'd showered together. I'd kissed her under the running water. I'd taken the soap, and I used it like my fingers, taking my time, touching every square inch of her skin, running lines over the ink on her skin. Thinking on it now had my body buzzing, had my cock growing hard. The curves of her body, the way she felt all sudsy and wet, was nothing short of amazing. One of the best moments of my life.

We didn't have sex. I didn't want to push for more when everything else had been so mind-blowing.

Amanda was it. The girl of my dreams.

I don't know how I ever mistook love with Emma or anyone else. Because every one of my relationships before Amanda paled in comparison to what I felt now. I could wait. I felt like we should wait before we had sex again. Get to know each other more. Dig deeper into what this was. I had a fear of misconnecting again. I wouldn't jeopardize everything with Amanda by screwing up sex with her for a third time. So for now, torturous showers would have to be it for us.

"Hi," she whispered.

I'd woken her somehow.

"Hi."

"Mmmm, it's way too early."

"I know. I gotta go, though."

"No. Stay." She rolled into me, stretching an arm over my chest. She nestled her face into my ribs. "I love you, Nick." She said it out loud, so effortlessly. "I love you."

I laid there on my back, breathing hard, heart pounding. "Say it again," I muttered.

"I love you."

Nothing had ever sounded so good. My heart went from happily racing to pounding mad, out of control. My hands, they started tingling. I could hear the blood rushing in my ears.

Holy fuck, not now!

Of all moments, why now?!

I sat up, pulling away from her, burying my face in my hands. My hands—I couldn't stop them from shaking. I couldn't stop the feeling of pins and needles. They burned. I made a noise in my throat, a groan, because this wasn't fair. So far from fair. Once, in college, I'd been with a girl, and I had her in bed with me the next morning, just like this, and she witnessed one of my panic attacks. The girl got out of bed and left so fast, probably writing me off as crazy. Never texted me back again. Just ghosted me.

Amanda had seen my panic attacks before. But what the fuck would she think about this one? Because it was coming fast and hard and right after she said 'I love you' to me.

But I couldn't dwell on her. I couldn't have focused on her even if I wanted to. Because the only emotion I felt was intense, crippling fear, and it hit me like a freight train in my chest. I struggled to catch even one decent breath. Then came the tears. I sobbed like a child, tears blurring my vision. This panic attack was ten times more intense than the others she'd witnessed. I had nowhere to go. No place to hide. No control whatsoever. My shame, the full extent of my mental illness, was on display for her to witness.

The next several minutes were a blur. A huge blur. When some normalcy finally returned, I felt her close to me, hanging on to my arm.

"I'm sorry. I'm so sorry, Nick."

I blinked and blinked. I'd blacked out for a minute. Because truthfully, I could barely remember the last few minutes.

She was crying, sobbing herself.

So I knew it must have been bad. One of my worst.

"Nick, I'm so sorry."

I pulled away and got out of bed. Where were my clothes? "Don't apologize," I scolded. I found my pants on the floor. Stumbling, clearing my throat, I pulled them on. "Don't apologize, you did nothing."

"I never know what to do. I don't know if I should call 911. Nick, I've never been so scared. Nick, look at me."

I couldn't look at her. I felt so ashamed. So embarrassed. I was absolutely disgusted with myself. I couldn't be normal for even two seconds? Two fucking seconds? This beautiful, naked, sexy woman had me in her bed, telling me she loved me, and that was my reaction?

I hated myself.

"Nick. Look at me."

"I have to go."

"Dammit, Nick."

I lifted my eyes. Her tits—her pink, round, puffy, pregnant nipples. Her swollen little belly—swollen with our baby. The flowers swirling on her skin. Her face. Red. Stained with tears. "I love you," she said to me. Again. After everything I just put her through.

"You too," I said to her. It was all I could manage right now. I grabbed my shirt off the floor.

And I left.

~ CHAPTER 41 ~

AMANDA

It took me all morning to get out of bed. And even longer to get ready for work. Eventually, I made it in, about two hours after I'd been scheduled to start. John wasn't in today, thank God, and Finn barely blinked at my late arrival.

"Yo," he said to me.

"Yo," I said back.

"You look nice."

"Thanks."

I dropped my bag on the counter. I'd spent the morning blow drying my hair, curling it, and doing my makeup. I needed one hell of a distraction after Nick's panic attack and brisk departure this morning. And getting all glammed up had helped, if only a little.

"You ready for tonight?"

"Ready for what?"

"Dinner."

You know what? Finn looked nice too. He wore a button up shirt, sleeves rolled up to the elbows. His hair was styled, which was a pleasant surprise since half the time he rolled into work like he'd just rolled out of some girl's bed. "Dinner?"

"Lou invited me over for dinner. I'm heading there straight from work. Nick's mom is in town." Finn squinted at me, crossing his arms over his chest. "Wait, is this news to you?"

"His mom!"

"Yeah, she showed up from Maine yesterday. Mrs. Jasmine and Nick's niece, Samantha are staying at Nick's house. I met them both yesterday, sort of, through the door with Lou. She invited me to dinner tonight. I'm flipping the fuck out though. Lou and I haven't even met in person yet. We've just been talking through the door. Well, more recently we upgraded to a window. So I'm excited to see her face-to-face, but also I'm scared to death. We have great chemistry through doors. Do you think that means we still will have the same chemistry without the door? It worked for those people on Love Is Blind, right?"

I squeezed my eyes shut, trying to process. "I don't think I'm invited. Nick never mentioned this."

"Nick's mom said you were coming too. You and Nick. I think it's going to be super casual. Just dinner at his house."

"I need to go. I need to take the day off." I grabbed my bag from the counter, backing away. "I'm too pregnant for this shit." Before Finn could say anything else, I had my bag over my shoulder and was pushing out the door.

I didn't go home.

I went to the pier. I needed a day off. I needed some time to relax. I needed my dad's friend Bobby, whom I knew would be at the pier. Like always. So I headed there, to sit and fish with him today. Nothing else. No more drama. I needed peace. Just peace today.

~ CHAPTER 42 ~

NICK

The thing about my panic attacks, especially the one I had this morning, was that they were exhausting. Exhausting and often debilitating. Today was my very first day back at work at the North Carolina Aquatic Preservation Society, and it felt like I'd taken eight Benadryl for breakfast and someone had asked me to operate heavy machinery. I blindly went through the motions. I did my best to appear normal. I wore my beanie all day for security, even though it was June now and increasingly hard to pass off as 'cool.'

When I finished work later that evening, I felt like the *Walking Dead*. I even tripped on the cement on my way out to my car. I wasn't even sure how safe it was for me to drive back to Amanda's.

I'd been neglecting my mom. I'd sent her a text message yesterday, saying I was staying the night at Amanda's. Today I wanted to do the same. But if I was going to cancel on her again, I felt I owed her at least a phone call. So, squinting into the sinking sun, I dialed her number.

She picked up after one ring.

"Mom? Hello? Hey, it's Nick."

"There you are Nick, finally," she said over the phone. "I've been trying to reach you all day."

"I've been at work."

"I know. So dinner is at 7. Don't be late."

I had to pinch my eyes shut. "What?"

"Dinner. Remember, dinner. I wanted to meet your girlfriend and Lou's boyfriend. Finn's already over here. He's such a gentleman. So handsome too." I could picture Finn standing right in front of her as she gushed over him. "He told me Amanda knows about dinner. He told her earlier today at work. He just called her to confirm. He said she's on her way."

"Fuck, Mom!"

"Nick! Language, please."

"I'm sorry. But Mom, I hate you a little right now for this."

"Oh, you'll get over it. Oh!" I heard a noise in the background, a knock at the door followed by some commotion over the line. "Oh hello," I heard Mom saying. "You must be Amanda. It's so nice to meet you, honey. Come in, come in."

"Mom. Mom!"

Nothing.

"Mom!"

She was ignoring me, so I hung up. Shit. I fumbled the phone in my hands, shoving it in my pocket. Amanda was there, at my house. She went to meet my mom and I wasn't even there! I had to get there. My exhaustion vanished, replaced with adrenaline, as I hurried for my car. I jumped in the driver's seat like the cops were after me, started the engine, and drove as fast as I could manage straight for my rental house.

I was going to lose her—*fucking lose* the girl of my dreams. Between my panic attacks, being forced to meet my mother, and all the bad sex I'd been giving her lately—she'd be gone for sure. I'd bored Emma to death. That other girl had ghosted me before I ever even learned her name. And I was certain Amanda would be my next casualty.

I made it to the house a minute later. With my laptop bag from work over my shoulder, I barreled up the stairs two at a time, busting in through the front door.

On the other side, everyone was all calm, all smiles, all polite. The air felt light. The mood even lighter. How did my mom do it? Every garden party she'd ever hosted on our family's luscious lawn back home looked exactly like this.

Preppy, polished, and fake as hell.

Amanda was in a blouse. Soft material. Ivory colored. It did two things—hid her tattoos and her stomach. She had a glass of lemonade filled with ice in her hand. Clear evidence of my mom. And Finn—ew, his hair was shiny with hairspray. He wore a button up shirt, the guy taking a play out of Amanda's playbook, also covering most of his tattoos. Then there was Lou. She looked like she'd washed her hair today. Good for her.

I took a breath, locking my fingers on top of my head, feeling the fabric of my knit hat.

"Just in time," Mom said to me, coming into the living room from the kitchen with a plate of what looked to be bacon-wrapped scallops. Her blonde hair was styled meticulously around her round face, as usual. "You look sweaty, honey. Why don't you go wash up? Dinner won't be ready for at least thirty more minutes."

"Hi, Nick," my niece Samantha said, as she hopped off the couch. She gave me the cutest, quickest, shyest hug.

"Hi, Sam."

It was hard to be annoyed seeing her face. She moved back to the couch. This had to be especially awkward for her. That was my mom's specialty—making teenagers feel awkward. "I'm just going to go wash up then," I muttered. "Amanda. Come with me?"

She nodded. "Excuse me," she said to the others. Then she followed, all calm, all quiet, down the hallway. She stepped with me into my room.

"Fuck," I said the moment the door clicked closed behind us.

I dropped my laptop bag on the floor.

She didn't say anything. She only stepped deeper into my room. I noticed she had on flats—like the dress shoes women sometimes wore. I'd only ever seen her in sneakers. Her makeup was soft, her hair tied back, and she barely looked like the girl I loved. Not that this was a bad look on her. I just wasn't sure it felt natural. "What are you doing, Amanda?"

"I showed up for dinner."

"I'm sorry about that."

"No, it's fine. How are you?" She picked at her fingernails avoiding my eyes. "I've been worried."

"I'm okay."

"Has another happened since?"

"No. They don't happen back to back. I should be good for a few days."

"You terrified me."

I breathed in deep. "I know."

"Your mom is nice."

"Yeah. She's alright. Most of the time." Her eyes were still on her nails instead of me. "You look nice. Different, it's not my favorite look on you, but nice."

"Um. Thanks, I guess."

Crap. I pulled off my hat, tossing it onto my dresser. This wasn't going well. I ran my hands through my hair. "I mean—"

"Nick, I should get back out to the living room so nobody thinks we're back here doing something we shouldn't be doing."

"Right. Right. You're right."

"Okay." She stepped toward my bedroom door. She had to pass me to escape. I could see it on her face—she didn't want to be here. She'd rather be in the living room with my overbearing mother than be stuck back here with me. She probably thought of me as a emotional ticking time bomb. Which, essentially, was exactly what I was. "Hey," I said when she was close, stopping her before she could walk out. "Nobody's ever shown up like this for me. It means everything to me that you're here."

"It's just dinner."

"No, it's not. Thank you, and you look beautiful. Really, you do."

Her eyes found mine. "Not your favorite look though."

"Well, my favorite look is you naked in bed. Your hair down, all sexy and wild. Your nipples showing. But I know I can't have my way all the time."

A cute little smirk moved over her lips. There. Yes. It was the best damn thing ever. A little color even came to her cheeks. "You could if you wanted," she whispered.

"Really?"

"Yes."

I felt warm all over despite the fact that we were basically in the middle of a dinner party—one of the things I hated most in this world. I touched her face. I touched my forehead to hers. It felt so good just being near her. She rested her hands on my chest. Maybe she wasn't in as much of a rush to get away from me as I thought.

"You were on my mind all day," I muttered quickly, knowing we only had another minute alone. "You and your pregnant nipples."

"What? Oh God."

Her hands raised to cover her face. I'd embarrassed her. I hadn't meant to. I gently pulled her hands away. "I meant... I can tell a difference. In the light this morning, I really got a chance to see you naked. I love it. I love the difference. I love being the reason behind that difference. You're so beautiful; what I did to you this morning almost broke me in half. I'm sorry for what I put you through. We need to have a real conversation about my panic attacks. Not now, but eventually."

She nodded.

"I'll be just one minute. I'm just going to take a thirty second shower. Sit with Sam until I get back. She's safe."

"I can handle myself. I'll be fine on my own. Take as long as you need in the shower."

Amanda stepped away, out my bedroom door. The moment she was gone, I hurried to get undressed. I needed to be on my best game for this dinner. I couldn't fuck it up.

~ CHAPTER 43 ~

AMANDA

Nick had so much natural charisma; he practically oozed it out of his eyeballs. After he showered and dressed, he joined everyone at the dinner table. He smiled easily. He conversed with his mom as if they were old friends. The guy from this morning, the one who cried uncontrollably in my bed—where was he? Because if I didn't know better, I'd say this wasn't the same man.

It made me think that his mom likely knew nothing of his panic attacks. Or panic disorder, as I'd heard Nick call it. He kept it hidden from her, and I'm guessing from his dad too. Which seemed like an enormous thing to hide from your parents for however many years he'd been hiding it.

But I knew. And knowing it about him suddenly felt like a privilege. Like he'd let me peak beneath his 'handsome charismatic guy' facade.

He'd sure terrified me this morning though. I told him I loved him and it sent him straight into a panic attack. I'd dwelled on that all day. I'd been worried for him, even a little angry at him for it, felt insecure with myself.

But here he was, clutching my hand under the table, telling me minutes ago how much he liked my pregnant nipples, of all things, and now he was telling his mom all about the turtle tattoo I'd put on his ass. He told her like he was proud of it. It made me look at his earlier panic attack a little differently. It was suddenly a lot less frightening. His panic attacks were a part of him. They didn't define him. Or control him. Just one small piece of the guy I loved.

"Amanda did it. She's incredibly talented."

"I need to see this tattoo," his mom insisted. "Where is it?"

"My butt, Mom. You can't see it."

"I've seen your bottom before."

"Well, you haven't seen my adult ass."

"I've seen it," Finn chimed in. "I was there the day Nick first came in and Amanda put it there. It's nice. Why don't you show everyone?"

Samantha giggled.

"Thanks, Finn. But no."

"So." His mom grabbed her lemonade and sat back in her chair. Her eyes were on me. "If I can't see the tattoo, then Amanda, tell me more about when you two first met. What'd you think of Nick? First impression."

Oh God. So far, I'd kept quiet and reserved. I let go of Nick's hand, resting my own above the table, giving his mom my complete attention. *Well, here goes nothing.* "Honestly, at first I didn't like him much. I thought he seemed cocky and privileged, and what kind of guy comes in wanting a turtle on his ass? But he smelled really good. Like insanely good, he always does. I'll give him that. My job is to get up close and personal with people's skin, so smelling them is part of my job. I actually don't like how most people smell. Most wear too much perfume or too much cologne, or they don't bathe enough. Or maybe it's their natural smell I don't like. It's something I've always been weird about. I think my sense of smell is much more enhanced than most people's. Or I'm pickier than most people about smell. But Nick, he smelled damn good."

Crickets.

Great.

I had the whole table's attention. They were all staring at me. I thought I was being funny, sort of, but my smell talk got little reaction out of everyone. Except Nick. I noticed he had a small smile on his handsome lips. "Anyway. He smelled good. He was easy to talk to. I didn't sleep that night. We stayed up the whole night together until John came in the next morning. Then Nick left for Maine. That was that. I didn't think I'd ever see him again. But Nick came back to the shop when he returned to town."

"Yes. *Kill Devil Ink* was the first place we stopped," Lou added, her voice so gentle and kind. "Nick had to go there first."

At least one person seemed pleased with my story, supportive even.

His mom—she was harder to read. Did she like me? Did she dislike me? I couldn't tell. Did she know I was pregnant?

Had Nick told her?

Because there were two reactions a woman like her would have to something like that. *Yay, I'm going to be a grandma.* Or... *hell no, I don't want this hussy having my grandbabies.*

In which category did this woman fall?

I stayed fairly quiet for the rest of the meal. I let Nick and Finn carry the conversation. I ate the incredible meal Mrs. Jasmine had cooked. I drank her lemonade. But if she didn't like me, if something about my job or the way Nick met me didn't please her, then I wasn't about to bend over backward to kiss her ass.

Her attention shifted to Finn and Lou. When Finn told her about how they met, how they'd been talking every day through the closed door, she laughed and smiled, giggled almost, and that was when I decided—no, this woman didn't like me.

Dinner ended. I offered to help with the dishes. Mrs. Jasmine denied my help.

"I'm going to go," I whispered to Nick. The others were setting up to play some kind of card game. I loved card games, but I couldn't stay any longer. My introvert heart wanted to retreat.

"I'll go with you."

"No, stay. Don't leave because of me."

"Am I invited over tonight?" he whispered, his blue eyes on me.

God, yes. "Always, Nick."

"Then I'm fucking leaving right this minute with you. Mom," he called out loudly across the room. "Dinner was great. We're leaving. See you tomorrow."

Mrs. Jasmine hurried out of the kitchen, drying her hands on a towel. She frowned but didn't argue with Nick. "Okay. I'll see you tomorrow." She hugged him, squeezing him hard, kissing his cheek. For me, I got a handshake. "Nice to meet you, Amanda."

"You too," I answered politely.

A minute later, we stepped outside. "Maybe you should stay. Your mom's here all the way from Maine and you've been with me most of that time."

He breathed in deeply like it was his first bit of fresh air all day. "You couldn't pay me to go back inside."

"Nick—"

"Amanda, do you know how often I do what other people want?" He touched a piece of my pink hair that had fallen loose from the updo twist I'd attempted. "All the damn time. All I want right now is to be with you, at your house, in your bed. I get it if you'd rather me stay because of my, you know, *instability*. I get that. But don't make me stay when you want me there, too. Because your house is the only place I want to be right now."

His words washed through me. He didn't even care that my house was crappy. That it was too small, needed so many repairs, and couldn't hold a candle to his rental. He didn't care that his mom didn't like me. He didn't even seem to notice it.

"You can come over on one condition."

"Name your price."

I stared up at him, stuck on his handsome face, mesmerized by those eyes, a little weak in the knees over how crazy I was over this man. "You make love to me. Or. I mean, you *properly* fuck me." I felt my face flush. "Deal?"

"Go get in my car."

"Was that a deal?"

"Yes, go get in my car." He made a noise in his throat and he touched his forehead to mine. His fingers unbuttoned my top button of my blouse. Then the next. Then the next. "I will *properly* fuck you all night long. I promise."

~ CHAPTER 44 ~

NICK

This woman. Amanda was under my skin, in my hair, and floating through my veins. I needed inside her. I needed closer to her. I wanted the night she'd made me promise her. But my need was also muddied with my anxiety. Anxiety, for me, was like this annoying third wheel I would never be rid of. If I had another panic attack tonight, I'd never forgive myself.

After we drove to her house, after she opened the door and let me in, I moved to kiss her. That was what she wanted, right? That was the natural next step, right?

"Hold on," she said to me, touching my chest, stopping me. "I'll be right back."

"Okay." I took a step back.

She moved through her house, disappearing into her kitchen.

I took a moment, slipped off my shoes, and turned on one of the table lamps in her living room. I gave myself a little pep talk while I waited. *It's just Amanda. You can be fucking normal for this.*

She came back, something in her hand. "Here. Before I forget," she said to me. She walked up beside me in her living room and handed me her spare key. It was the same key I'd been using each night to get in her house. The one she normally kept outside under the doormat in the back. "You can have this."

I took it from her fingertips. My own keys were in my pocket. I pulled them out, and I added her single silver key to the rest of mine. "What do you want this to mean?" I asked. I gently tossed my set of keys, complete now with her key, onto the couch. Then I followed with my cell phone, pulling it from my other pocket, getting rid of it too.

"I don't know. I didn't really think it through. Don't read into it too much."

"Hmm." I touched the edge of the fabric of her blouse. Earlier I'd unbuttoned a couple of the buttons. They still were unbuttoned, showing a hint of her perfect body underneath. I undid the next button in the line. "I'm going to read into it, Amanda. I'm going to read *the hell* into it."

"What—what will you read it as?"

I undid another button, another, and then the last. I moved the material aside brushing my fingers over her round, pregnant stomach. It was still little enough to hide, like she had done today, but round enough to really see it when you had the sort of vantage point I now had. "I'm reading it as an open invitation into your bed every night." I moved to the couch. Still touching her stomach, I brought my lips to where I knew our baby was somewhere underneath.

"You pretty much already have that."

"I'll read it as I can come over now a little earlier than midnight each night. Maybe catch you for dinner sometimes. Maybe leave my toothbrush here. Maybe, finally, get your phone number." I took a breath, hoping I wasn't terrifying her. Because I wasn't terrifying myself at all. I wanted to take this next step with her. I wanted it all with her. "Hi baby," I whispered to her stomach before I sat back against the couch cushion.

"Okay," Amanda said. "I can't."

Can't what?

I don't know what sparked fire in her, but Amanda ignited. She peeled off her shirt the rest of the way. She kicked off her flats and shimmied down her pants. Hell, her underwear too.

"Take off your pants," she whispered. "Take off your shirt."

She didn't have to tell me twice. I grabbed my shirt from behind and yanked it off over my head. I tossed it aside as she unhooked her bra, pushing it away, showing off her beautiful tits. Then I worked down my pants, kicking them off, just as Amanda, naked now, straddled my lap. She settled in against me, warm and wide open, as she grabbed my face, digging her fingers into my hair.

She kissed me hard. She kissed me with passion, with angst, with hunger. "I love you," she said against my mouth. "I'm so in love with you." She squeezed her arms around my neck. She gave me more of her kisses. Not just my mouth—my face, my jaw, my neck. "I love you," she said again.

It was my 'hi baby' comment that ignited this spark, I realized. I saw a glimpse of this fire when she interrupted my shower yesterday. She was always so strong, confident, and independent. This was her vulnerability, translated into love, on full display.

I took her face in my hands, so she'd slow down. "Hey, I love you too."

She had tears in her eyes.

I hadn't meant to make her cry.

"I'm going to take care you. You and our baby. I promise."

"Good. Keep proving that."

"I will."

I would. I really would. She'd never given me many details on her past relationships. I'd never asked. But someone, at some point, had hurt her. I'd never thought that of her before. I'd never seen it until now. She kept that pain well hidden. Whereas, with Emma, I think I wore my pain on my sleeve. Not anymore. Amanda had taken that pain away for me. I wanted to do the same, take any of hers away too.

I adjusted under her. I brought the head of my cock into position against her opening. I pushed inside. She moved on top of me, helping to guide my full length all the way in. "Yes, Nick! Oh God, yes!"

I closed my eyes.

She felt so damn good.

So wet. So warm.

She started to move, riding me, working her hips, coming up and down hard on my cock. "Fuck, woman. I love you." I tipped my head back, smiling, enjoying this beautiful woman who had my whole heart, who I think loved my crazy just as much as she loved my calm, cool, and collected self. She wouldn't be here right now if she didn't love both sides to me.

After another moment, I snapped open my eyes. It was my turn. I moved, pushing her body down onto the couch cushions so I could be on top, so I could do the work. My fingertips dug into her colorful thighs and pushed her legs wider, sinking inside her this way.

Then I went crazy on my girl. Fucking her the same way I had our first night together. Without control. Without worry. Without anxiety. I felt her flesh, breathed in her scent, and soaked in the moment. Then I touched her clit to get her to scream. When I felt her let go, when I knew I had her at my full mercy, I slowed down. Now I kissed her softly.

I kept strumming my fingers over her wetness, while pulsing carefully, easy, gentle strokes inside her. The moment seemed to last and last. And when she finally came down off that high, I let go. I came inside her. Nothing had ever felt so raw, so right, so real.

Thoroughly exhausted now, the entire day catching up with me, I collapsed on the couch beside her. I inched her body over so I could fit beside her on the couch without falling to the floor.

She curled into my chest. "Careful, Nick. Or I might ask you to move in with me next."

I smiled.

I felt sleep drifting over me fast.

"If you asked, I would say yes."

"You're bullshitting me."

"No, I'm not."

"Then move in with me."

"Okay."

~ CHAPTER 45 ~

AMANDA

The next few days were a blur. Of work. Of sex. Of Nick. I was working more than usual because I needed the extra money before this baby came. But when I wasn't at work, and when Nick wasn't at work, we were back at my house, in my bed, or in today's case, on the kitchen table. Maybe it was part of my pregnancy hormones, but I couldn't get enough of my handsome man.

He seemed to be having a similar problem, because in the middle of cooking dinner, he'd whispered, *"lay down on the table."* We'd finished now. My skin still tingled in the aftermath. I eased off the wooden tabletop, adjusting the gym shorts I'd changed into after work, feeling shy as hell. We hadn't even bothered undressing that time. We'd barely even said hello.

Nick grabbed two glasses from one of my cabinets and ran both under the tap water at my sink. He handed me one, while he drank from the second. He smiled at me while he took a sip. His blue eyes drifted down my body.

"Stop," I said to him.

"What?"

"Stop. Focus on dinner."

"Shit, dinner." He set down his glass, rushing to the pan that was sizzling on the stove. "I burned it." He moved the pan off the hot burner and turned off the stove. "Sorry, that was my fault. I got distracted when you came into the kitchen in those shorts."

"The crappy gray shorts I wear to bed turned you on?" *The ones I'd owned half my life? The only ones lose enough to fit my pregnant belly?*

"Yes."

"I'll have to wear them more often then."

"No. I'll never get anything done."

At his words, I couldn't help myself. I wrapped my arms around his waist from behind. I squeezed him hard while he worked to sort out our burnt dinner. He meant everything to me. I kept getting this feeling lately—that the night he got me pregnant was divine intervention or something crazy. Maybe my dad up in heaven was watching out for me, and he sent Nick my way somehow. Because, holy shit, was I happy I had him. I was intensely happy I had him to go through this pregnancy with. I didn't know him that first night we'd slept together. For all I knew, he could have been some psycho. Instead, as it turned out, he was this wonderfully sweet, caring man who, literally, always put me first. His mom was in town. And still, he was always home with me by dinner time each night. Always staying over. Always giving me—everything.

"Amanda, please let go."

I dropped my hands from his waist immediately. "Sorry."

"Fuck, it's happening. My hands are tingling." He turned away from the stove. He sat on the floor with his legs close to his chest, an uncomfortable-looking position for him. "Amanda." His breathing turned heavy now, strained as he spoke. "Go—for a few minutes. Just go watch an episode of that show you've been watching. I'll come get you when it's passed. You don't need to stay for this."

I knelt down next to him.

He hadn't had a panic attack since the morning he cried in my bed and scared me half to death. He even commented this morning how it had been almost a week and he was about due. He had tears in his eyes now, just the same as that morning, as he gave me a silent plea. Those tears made his eyes just about the most brilliant color of blue I'd ever seen. My heart was breaking for him. It was insane to see such a strong, otherwise happy, confident man like him weakened within seconds.

"Go," he muttered.

I wasn't going anywhere.

I sat beside him on the floor. We both had our backs to the cabinets. I didn't say anything as I listened to his breathing and his groans. Tears tried to blur my vision, but I fought them off. I knew I couldn't let him see me emotional when it finished. I had to be strong for him. After a few minutes, his breathing calmed, which I knew meant the worst of it was over.

"Fuck," he whispered. He rested his head back against the cabinet behind us. "Fuck. What if I do that when I'm in the middle of watching the baby? You're not home. I'm all alone. And that happens. I can't be trusted with a baby."

"If it happens—you put the baby down somewhere safe. Where it can't roll off a bed, or changing table, or whatever. Then you wait for it to pass. If the baby has to cry for a minute, it will be okay."

He made a noise deep in his throat. "Fuck, Amanda. I'm sorry I'm not better for you."

"I don't want better. I just want you. Go. You should go rest now."

He told me the other day how tiring his panic attacks usually were. How afterwards, he felt this wave of straight exhaustion. He'd said that after an attack he could usually sleep for twelve straight hours.

"I'll order some takeout, since I'm fairly sure dinner is inedible by now, and when it gets here, I'll come to bed too."

"Yeah," he muttered.

He stood, and I stood with him.

He wasn't making eye contact anymore. He'd been practically eye-fucking me minutes before, so this was a stark difference—one I did not like and wasn't going to tolerate. I grabbed his face. I stood on my toes so I could be closer to his height because he really needed to hear what I was about to tell him. "You're everything to me. I wake up every day with a dumb, silly smile on my face, because of you. I know you've seen it. It's ridiculous. I'm embarrassed by how ridiculous I know that smile looks. I'm excited to be a mom because of you. That isn't going to change for me because of one panic attack. Because of ten. Because of a million. So don't be harsh on yourself. Don't ever doubt my feelings for you. And don't you dare ask me to leave again. Because I'm not going anywhere."

"Damn, Amanda," he muttered. He swallowed; his jaw tight. "Damn."

"Go. Seriously."

"Yes, ma'am." Then I saw it. The trace of a small smile on his handsome lips.

I softly kissed those lips.

"Rest. Let me worry about dinner for once." He was always insisting on cooking for me.

"Okay. Join me in a little bit."

"I will."

He moved to kiss me. I mean, *really* kiss me. He pressed his forehead against mine, breathed in deeply as his hands came gently to my neck, and he kissed me. It was brief, but it was fire. "Love you, baby."

Then he dropped his hands away and left the kitchen.

I let out a breath.

Fuck, I loved him.

~ CHAPTER 46 ~

NICK

"Your mother is here."

"What?"

"She's at the door."

Not the first words I want to wake up to in the morning.

I rubbed at my eyes. Sunshine lit up Amanda's bedroom. She stood beside the bed. Her figure, the small bump of her belly under her shirt, was on display in the sunlight. She was really, no matter the day, no matter the circumstances, the best thing to wake up to. Even if she was telling me my mother was here.

Memories of last night came to me. For a second, I'd forgotten that I'd had another panic attack. I remembered now. As far as my attacks went, this one had been relatively mild. But annoyingly, it had happened right after sex. Right when Amanda had her arms around my middle. I hated that my anxiety controlled so much of my life. At least with Amanda, one of the best things about her—I couldn't seem to scare her off, bore her to death, or drive her straight into the arms of the next waiting Rockstar.

"My mom?" I cleared my throat.

"Yeah. I answered the door in this." She gestured to her clothing.

"Well, fuck." Amanda wore a tight-fitting shirt that showed exactly how pregnant she was. "I was going to have to tell her eventually. Might as well get it over with today." I climbed out of bed. Gathering my clothes off the floor, I started to get dressed.

"She hates me," Amanda muttered.

"What? She doesn't hate you."

"She *really* hates me."

"No way. She loved my brother Mick from the start when he wasn't even her own. Trust me, I don't see any reason why she wouldn't love you."

Amanda pointed at her stomach. "This reason."

"Not a reason," I said, yanking on my shirt and slipping on my sneakers all in one skilled motion. The thing about my mom was—she had two categories. She either loved a person. Or she hated that person with a fiery passion. I would not let her put Amanda into the latter category. Besides, Raven, my brother's wife, I'm pretty sure used to be a prostitute. Like no joke, an actual prostitute. Mick brought her home one day and my mother welcomed the woman with open arms. I wouldn't tolerate her doing anything less with Amanda. "Give me a minute to speak with her. I'll see what she wants."

Amanda nodded.

She was quiet, clearly upset by something my mom might have already said. I touched her chin and kissed her lips briefly. Then I left. My mom would not dare to fuck with me right now.

"Yes," I said opening Amanda's front door. I stepped outside into the dewy morning air. "Did you need to come over this early in the morning, making a scene, Mom?"

It didn't matter that the sun was barely over the horizon; Mom looked impeccable. Her hair and makeup fresh, her outfit a portrait of too many layers. This wasn't Maine. She didn't need to dress like it was. "I did. Your girlfriend, *of how many weeks,* is pregnant."

Well, shit. I guess she did know.

That reminded me. Amanda's ultrasound was today. The one where we finally would find out the sex of the baby. It was a good thirty-minute drive to the ultrasound place on the mainland. We probably needed to be getting ready for that instead of dealing with this right now.

"I'm aware she's pregnant."

"And you were going to tell me—*when*? I've been in town, staying in your rental, having dinner with Lou every night for over a week now. Waiting, mind you, for you to tell me since that very first day I meet Amanda. Today is my last day. I leave tomorrow. A fact you would know if you had bothered spending any time with me this past week. And I'm forced to confront you about it like this. A mom shouldn't have to do that, Nick."

"You knew when we had dinner?"

"Yes. A girl like Amanda with her pink hair and tattoos doesn't normally wear a lose-fitting blouse like the one she had on. So I thought, why? Just for me? Doesn't take a rocket scientist to figure she might be hiding her figure. Plus, that blouse, a little too sheer for hiding anything. I don't like people who hide things. Doesn't sit well with me."

"You arrived out of nowhere. You invited her to dinner, kind of behind my back. We didn't have a minute to even discuss telling you or plan how to tell you before you pushed dinner on us. We weren't trying to hide her pregnancy. But I guess you know now. So... surprise! You're going to be a grandma."

"Don't be a smart ass."

"I'm not."

"Does Mick know?"

"I haven't told anyone."

"I thought you would have at least told Mick. But I guess not since he barely hears from you, either…"

I groaned. *Here we go.* I was about to hear all her grievances. "Mom," I warned.

"Your brother is not about to say it. But he misses you. Your father and I miss you. We supported you the first time you moved to North Carolina and perused your turtles. But now… when are you coming home, Nick? And for good?"

"Well I'm about to have a fucking baby, Mom. Do you think I'm planning on moving at the moment?"

She cringed at my language. I didn't normally swear around her. In fact, I didn't normally speak my mind with her. All my life, I'd pretty much kept quiet, let them run things for me. My degree in Marine Biology had been my first step away from them. My move to North Carolina, the second. It wasn't that I didn't love them. It was that I felt suffocated around them.

"I'm not moving back anytime soon. I feel good around this girl."

"Good how? Explain?"

"Happy. I'm happy."

"But are you healthy?" Mom sighed. She rested her hands on her plump hips. She knew a little about the extent of my panic attacks. When she had first witnessed one, the summer after my freshman year of college, she put me straight into therapy.

With *her* therapist.

"Have they increased or decreased?"

She never spoke of my panic attacks. And if she had to, it was like this. Never putting a name to them.

"Same. Maybe slightly more often. But what does that have to do with anything?"

"The person you're with should be a calming force. She should be lessening your anxiety. Not heightening it by being dumb enough to let herself get pregnant. Babies, trust me, are the very definition of anxiety. I look at this house and all I see is anxiety. Between the overgrown lawn and the roof that likely leaks when it rains… Anyway, how far along is she?"

"Mom. I can't have this conversation with you. Not right now. Not today."

Speaking of anxiety—I could feel it bubbling under my skin, itching my neck, making my stomach feel a little like acid. Amanda was not my source of anxiety. At the moment, my mother was.

"It's not Amanda I don't like. She seems sweet. I'm just worried. I'm always going to worry about you. The further away from home you are, the more I worry. You know?"

"Yep."

"Alright. I'll go. Finn is taking us and Lou to the beach soon. He gives her less anxiety, you know, not more. And they're cute to watch."

Finn could go fuck himself. But I was happy Lou seemed to be enjoying spending her time with him. Going to the beach with him was an amazing step. And Finn being there for Lou lately meant I could be here with Amanda more.

Mom stepped down off Amanda's porch.

"Come say goodbye tonight," she called over her shoulder as she walked toward her rental car.

I lingered for a moment after she disappeared, collecting myself.

I was sweating, and not from the humidity.

I felt jittery and sick, and I knew if I stepped immediately inside Amanda would notice. I couldn't let her see that. So I waited. I waited until I had everything under control before I stepped back inside her house.

~ CHAPTER 47 ~

AMANDA

"We need to get going so we don't miss this ultrasound."

Nick's mom was long gone, and Nick was in my bathroom. He'd just finished brushing his teeth, and he looked at me through the reflection of the mirror. He looked so handsome standing there in my tiny, cramped bathroom. The tiles coating the walls were a dingy yellow color that clashed with the rich color of his dark hair.

"Did she say anything else to you?"

He'd been questioning me since she left.

"No. Nothing else." I gave him a small, and I'll admit forced, smile.

Nick wiped his mouth with a towel. Then he stepped past me. I was already ready to go. I'd showered and dressed. I grabbed my bag and followed him outside, getting into his car with him. I didn't say much as he started the ignition and we left for the clinic where I had my appointment. All week we'd been excited about this. Now the air felt thick, heavy with tension.

"After today, we should start buying stuff for the baby. I mean, we'll know if we should be buying boy stuff or girl stuff. Right? I haven't been in that other room in your house. The door is always closed. Is it a second bedroom?"

"Yes."

"Would it work for the baby?"

"I guess so."

Nick turned onto the main road. I smoothed my hands over my jean shorts, pulling at them. Maybe I should have tried to cover some of my tattoos for this ultrasound. Shorts and a tank-top, I decided, might have been an awful idea. I felt exposed. All my life, my tattoos had felt the opposite of that. In high school, I'd been quiet and shy. I never stood out. I wasn't popular or unpopular. I wasn't good or bad at sports. I'd always fallen in middle ground with basically everything I did. My tattoos gave me a little something extra—something special. They'd given me an edge up on everyone else. And they'd always felt like this protective layer I wore against the world. Something that made me not-so-average.

I felt judged today.

I felt not good enough for Nick all over again.

I felt the word his mom had used. She said I was trapping Nick. Trapping him here in North Carolina. That Nick was a good man and he would do everything he could to provide for me. Because that was his nature. But at what cost, she'd asked—his sanity?

I'd been wrong that night at dinner. She knew of his panic attacks, and of his anxiety. And I'd listened at the door while Nick spoke with her. I shouldn't have, but I had. I heard her question whether or not I was right for him. I made his anxiety worse, not better. This baby—it would make it worse, too.

"You okay?" he asked for like the fourth time.

"I'm nervous. Do you want it to be a boy or girl?"

I'd never asked him this. I'd never thought to.

"Either." He reached for my hand. He laced his fingers with mine. "Either," he repeated. "I'll be fucking happy either way." He tightened his grip. "I probably, as a twenty-three-year-old man, should be freaking the fuck out right now. I mean, we're a little young for a kid, right? That's what most people would be thinking right now, right? How old are you Amanda? I don't think I've ever asked."

"Twenty…Twenty-five," I stuttered.

I don't know why, but I always thought Nick was a bit older than me. How had we never talked about our ages? Probably because I spent so much time *not* talking to him in the beginning.

"I know the way I should feel about this," he said to me. "Scared. But I'm excited. Between you and the baby… I'm *really* fucking excited. And I know that's not normal. And I know with my anxiety I should be feeling a different way. But I look at you, and you're my hope. Hope in human form. Sorry—" He pulled his hand from my grip. And he cracked the window a little on his side, letting in some fresh air. "Sorry. It's hot in here."

"I can't believe you're younger than me." I picked at my fingernails.

"Why?"

"You don't seem younger. You're mature. You're rational. You know how to cook. You know how to get me off in bed. And you're right, most guys your age wouldn't be so excited about suddenly being a father. I assumed you were older because I usually only attract older men. Something about me appeals to older men. Maybe this air of mystery," I giggled. It sounded so ridiculous when I said it out loud. "I don't know. When I go to the grocery store, it's not guys my own age who try to talk to me. It's men who probably have a wife and kids at home. People look at me and see a certain type of person. And whoever that person is, she isn't the type who meshes up with your type of person." Now I wasn't even just talking about our ages. I was implying social differences too. "The guys I've dated in the past have always, all of them, been a disappointment. I don't really care about two years. I mean, two years is nothing. We're basically the same age. I just—I'm always surprised by you. In the best ways. And now I'm surprised again."

"I'm sure the men your same age or younger want to talk to you but are intimidated. Probably would piss their pants if a woman like you walked up to them in the grocery store and said hi. You might not be my normal type. Or who other people expect to be my normal type. But fucking trust me, my impulse tattoo was the best decision of my life."

Damn.

I had tears in my eyes.

"You mean that?"

"I mean that."

I loved him. I loved him so much. He always had a way of making me feeling amazing, even when I started the day feeling the opposite. He was good for me in so many ways. But was I good for him? His mom's words were still stuck in my head. Even as we made it to the ultrasound clinic. Even as we left the car and walked inside. Even as the technician put the gel   on   my   belly.

~ CHAPTER 48 ~

NICK

Amanda had her shirt pulled up to expose her bare stomach. Her stomach still wasn't noticeably big, but seeing her like that, it was obvious she was pregnant. I could tell she was nervous, or maybe still preoccupied with something my mom might have said earlier. She wasn't exactly herself, and I was having a hard time reading her. The technician squirted jelly on her skin and was now rolling the ultrasound wand across her stomach.

Our baby popped up on the screen.

With it came the sound of its heartbeat.

"That's it," the ultrasound technician said. "That's your baby."

Seeing and hearing made everything instantly ten times more real. I squeezed Amanda's hand. *Our baby!* That was our little baby. I'd never seen anything this incredible, this amazing. I suddenly understood when people called life a miracle. My own heart was racing out of control. The baby kept kicking on the screen. *Our baby!*

"Can you feel that?" the woman asked her.

"I think so. I wasn't sure if it was my stomach or the baby."

"It's the baby."

The baby was having the time of its life, putting on a show for us.

The technician began pointing out body parts, some more obvious than others. She took screenshots on her computer and seemed to be measuring different things. Then after a couple minutes—a couple minutes where I was in complete awe—she asked, "do you want to know the sex?"

"Yes," I said without hesitation.

"No," Amanda answered simultaneously.

What?

"Um." She stared at the technician's face. "Could you write it on a piece of paper and put it in an envelope for us?"

"Sure, honey," said the woman.

Okay, I guess we could find out later. Maybe Amanda wanted privacy when we found out. Maybe she wanted to do one of those gender reveal things. Maybe she simply wasn't ready to know yet. As the rest of the appointment continued, I tried not to worry on this, and instead simply enjoy the moment. But I had this small ball of fear growing inside me, and it was hard to push away.

The technician printed us some pictures. She made a copy of everything and downloaded it onto a disk. We took our souvenirs and left the office. It was hot today, stepping out of the building and into the North Carolina summer air. The sun beat on us. The humidity in the air was stifling. As we walked back to my car, I had to ask, "are you okay?"

"I'm good."

"Something feels a little off."

"I'm fine."

"Why didn't you want to know the sex of the baby?"

She shrugged. We reached my car. She stood at her door, pulled at the handle, but I hadn't unlocked it yet. I wasn't ready just yet to let this go. "You want to do one of those gender reveal things on social media? On your Instagram?" I still followed her there. But she only posted tattoos, not really much on her personal life. Maybe she had a second account I didn't even know about.

"God, no."

"Why the envelope then?"

Again, she shrugged.

Fuck.

Something was really wrong.

"What do you want to do today?" I tried.

"Can you just unlock the car?"

I unlocked it. She got inside, so I did the same on my side of the car. I buckled my seatbelt, started the engine, and got the air conditioning going. But I hesitated to start driving. "What do you want to do today?" I asked again. "I took the day off. We could go to lunch. It's almost time for lunch places to open."

"I think you should spend the day with your mom. She seemed upset that she hadn't seen you much since she's been here. She'd probably appreciate some of your time."

"She was going to the beach today with Lou and Finn. You want to do that?"

"No. No, I don't. But you go."

I took a breath. Sitting on a beach with my mom, Finn, and even Lou, sounded like torture. Amanda was the only person I wanted to spend time with today. "My mom has to understand that she can't just show up unannounced for an impromptu vacation. People have jobs and lives. They can't just drop everything to entertain her when she decides to show up.

She acts like she's doing other people a favor by visiting when in reality, it's just really fucking inconvenient." I took another breath. "Amanda, I live eight states away from her for a reason. I love her, but I can only take her in small doses."

"I think I just want to go home and rest today."

"Okay. We can do that."

"Alone, I mean. I need some time to think. I need some time to process everything. Is that okay?"

Christ. "Yeah, that's fine. I can drop you there. I can head into work today instead. It's not a big deal." I pulled my phone out of my pocket. I set the GPS back to her house. By the time I pulled into her driveway, I was sick to my stomach. She hadn't spoken the entire way home. I didn't know what was happening. Were we okay or not, or what? "Can I come back over later after work?"

"I'll call you," she said as she grabbed her bag off the floor of the car. "Bye, Nick. I love you."

That was it. That was the end of our conversation.

Had I done something wrong? She'd said, *I love you*. Maybe that meant we were fine. But I didn't feel fine. I felt pretty damn awful. Everything inside me wanted to follow her inside the house, demand some answers, get her to talk to me, but I didn't want to overreact if there was no need. Maybe she just needed a little space after today's appointment. Having this baby was a huge change. And it was her body having to accommodate that change. I wanted to respect whatever she needed at the moment. So I backed out of her driveway, I headed for work like I said I would, and I gave her the space I thought she needed.

~ CHAPTER 49 ~

NICK

Work sucked. But I went through the motions, I kept a smile on my face, and I got through it. I had a pit the size of Texas in my stomach when I left. Amanda hadn't called all day. I wasn't about to go back to my place tonight. Not a chance in hell. Instead, I went straight home to her house.

It's not like she hadn't given me a key.

Her car wasn't in the driveway when I arrived. I went inside looking for her anyway. "Amanda," I called out into her empty house.

No answer. Fuck.

I pushed my hands through my hair, breathing in a few deep breaths, and tried to keep my thoughts positive. Maybe she'd be home soon.

I called her number, but no answer.

I called *Kill Devil Ink*.

"Is Amanda in?" I asked when someone answered. I think it was John.

"Nah, she took the day off."

"Any idea where she might be?"

"No. Sorry, bye."

The line clicked dead.

I paced the living room. I could wait until she came home. But I knew myself. If I sat here long enough, stuck in my own thoughts, my emotions would run me over. I'd have a panic attack if I let my thoughts fester. I could already feel all that anxiety bubbling over in my stomach. And the simple truth was, Amanda could be at the grocery store for all I knew. Shopping for dinner for us. I stared at a framed photograph on her wall. It was of a pier, one of the many piers from the Outer Banks. I recognized the one in the photo because when I rode with the ATV riders, volunteering, I often passed this exact pier. There was a picture of Amanda and her father on this same pier on her desk at *Kill Devil Ink*.

Suddenly, this flash of realization hit me. She might be there. I don't know why, but I felt it. I knew how much her dad liked to fish. And I knew how much Amanda missed him sometimes. So I left and headed straight for the pier.

~ CHAPTER 50 ~

AMANDA

I sat on a bench at the end of Dad's favorite pier with the envelope from my ultrasound clutched in my hands. I stared at it. Inside were the results—the sex of the baby which was growing inside me. Yesterday, I'd been so excited to find out. But today, I had this enormous weight on me that wouldn't go away.

Bobby was on the corner of the pier. He stood with a few other older men, all of them I recognized. I'd said hi to him before I sat down. And now he chatted with the others. In the past, my dad would have been standing with them, talking with them, about the weather, about baseball, about whatever it was men talk about.

I wasn't going to open the letter without Nick. He deserved to know at the same time I did. But I knew, under different circumstances, after opening this letter, I would have raced here. I would have raced to tell my dad. I would never have done a 'gender reveal' like Nick had mentioned on social media. I just would have wanted to share the news with my dad. It mattered to me that he knew.

"Hey."

I don't know where he came from or how he knew I was here, but suddenly Nick was here. He sat down slowly beside me on the wooden bench. I could smell his fresh scent that I loved so much. It hit me solid in the chest. His shirt rippled against his chest in the breeze. Anything I'd been thinking moments ago was lost with him so close to my skin.

"Hey," he repeated. He leaned back against the boards.

"Hi."

"You going to open that?" He meant the envelope.

"No."

"Stare at it?"

"Yes."

"Okay."

I swallowed hard. I had pins and needles across my skin. I knew I'd been weird with him all day. But I worried that everything between us was magnified because of the baby. If the baby weren't part of our equation, would Nick love me with the same intensity? And then I had to wonder, was I even right for Nick?

"Do I make your anxiety worse?" I asked point blank. "Have your panic attacks increased since you came back to North Carolina? Since we got together?"

"You overheard my mom?"

"A little bit." I leaned forward on my knees. I felt nauseated. I knew the right thing to do would be to break up with him. End it amicably. Raise the baby together but separately. Be friends instead. Do whatever I could to not be added stress for Nick.

"What did she say that's bothering you?"

"She questioned if me and the baby were good for your sanity. I'm not so sure she's wrong."

He sighed and leaned forward on his knees close to me. "My mom knows nothing about my anxiety or what keeps me sane. I kept my panic attacks from her, from my family, all through high school. Then into college. She witnessed one and reacted by putting me in therapy. Like it was a magic cure. I know therapy is great for some people. But it only gave me more anxiety. I did learn one thing from therapy though: the source of my anxiety isn't external, it's internal. My anxiety comes from inside me."

His voice dropped.

"I create it. I put pressure on myself to be a certain way, to follow certain rules in social situations. I wish I didn't do all that, but I do and it's something I'm working on. I bottle up that anxiety until my body releases it. The baby is going to add stress. It's a baby and babies are stressful. I don't know how or if it will change the frequency of my panic attacks. But you.... Amanda, you're my sanity. My happiness. My hope. I love you. I would not normally admit this, but..." He breathed out a heavy breath and sat back. "Fuck," he whispered.

"What?" I pulled my legs up. My stomach felt as big as ever as I tried to turn toward him on the bench. "What, Nick?"

"My panic attacks… they're going to happen whether I'm with you or not. That's my reality. And it doesn't matter how old I get or how many I've already experienced, it still scares the shit out of me each and every time. It still brings me to my knees. It's still debilitating. It's still the worst moment of my life every time. But you, Amanda..." He touched my face. He moved his hands to my neck. "You... when you're close to me during one, it's kind of like an anchor in a storm. I don't like when people see me in those moments. I don't like when you see me like that." He pulled away. "But selfishly, I like when you're there. It's not so scary when you're there. You're the best thing for me. But I'm probably not the best thing for you, or for anyone. And I'm sorry for that."

He stood up.

Where was he going?

My heart raced, but the look on his face remained calm, and there was a calmness of the pier and laughter from all the men fishing a few yards away.

He started to walk away.

What did that mean? Did that mean we were over? I sat there and watched him, feeling my heart literally vibrate through my whole body. I stood up, grabbing the envelope, and raced after him. My steps were loud on the old wooden boards. I reached him and grabbed his hand, my fingers laced with his.

"Nick, don't go," I muttered. "You haven't met everyone."

"Who?"

"My dad's old friends. Come meet them."

"Sure. I would love to."

"Really?"

"Yes, I would love to."

"Okay, good." I smiled.

Each time he used the word 'love' it felt like he was saying he loved me. I squeezed his hand and he squeezed mine back. Then, as easy as that, he changed directions and started walking back with me, back toward Bobby and the other men. He met them all. He actually already knew some of them, including Bobby, from the ATV riders. He seemed causal and friendly with them, and I couldn't tell which version of Nick they were getting. My version or the version that acted a certain way for other people. It didn't matter. I relaxed as he spoke to them, and my heart returned to an even beat, because I realized he wasn't going anywhere, not if I wanted him to stay.

And I did want him to stay.

I wanted him to always stay.

As we walked away about half an hour later, the sun starting to sink on the horizon on the opposite side of the island, I said to him, "Thank you for getting that impulse tattoo. And for getting me pregnant. And for coming back to North Carolina. And for being just so fucking wonderful."

He stopped walking. He held my hand firmly so I'd stop with him.

I had tears in my eyes. I couldn't help it. I was a little embarrassed by it and didn't meet his eyes.

"As long as you want me with you, I'm not going anywhere," he said. He held my face in his hands so I'd look at him. "I'm serious. I'm always going to want that. I'm always going to be yours. You inked my heart when you inked my ass."

I couldn't help but smile.

"Sorry, that was cheesy." He smiled back at me.

"I liked it."

"Good. As long as you liked it."

He kissed me and wrapped his arms around me. Nothing had ever felt so real, so overwhelmingly right. I could feel how much he loved me, how much he cared, how there was no chance in hell he'd ever walk away as casually as he'd attempted before. I stood on my toes, grabbing on to his neck, just so I could get closer to him. I kissed him back equally. He was everything to me. Nothing else mattered but us and our baby. The rest of the world, including his mother, could go to hell. He was the best thing for me too.

"Open the envelope," he muttered once we parted. His cheeks were a little flushed.

"Now?"

"Sure. If you're ready."

I was, actually. Now was the perfect moment. I pulled the envelope from my pocket. I tore at the paper. I pulled out the small piece that the ultrasound technician had scribbled on. It had one word written on it.

Girl.

~ EPILOGUE ~

Seven Months Later

NICK

I couldn't breathe. *Now was not the time for this.* I was in the baby's closet, grabbing more wipes because there had been an explosion, when I felt that familiar rush of anxiety.

I sat to the floor.

I'd been seeing a specialist. One my mother was paying out of pocket for. One I had to drive all the way to Virginia Beach to visit. A few months back, I'd told her everything. I told her how many years I'd been struggling with my panic attacks and how her family therapist hadn't been what I needed. She was quick to research the best, and shell out the money needed to get me the real help required.

Turns out, having the *right* therapist helps.

I counted to ten. I pulled out this pocket compass thing I'd started carrying. It was an antique and something I'd found in Amanda's house when we'd done a very thorough, deep clean before the baby came. She thought it might have belonged to her grandfather or great-grandfather. She'd let me have it. And now it was my focus item.

I breathed in deep breaths through my mouth, I opened the lid of the compass, focused on the details, and I thought of Amanda. Her face the night I took her to a turtle hatching on the beach. Her excitement. Her thrill. I thought I was the only one who loved seeing baby turtles crawl from the sand to the water that much. Turns out, she loved it too. She made me take her to two others this past summer. Then I thought of Amanda the day the baby was born. Our little Mia. Of that feeling of pure joy we both shared the moment the baby arrived. I'd never experienced anything like it in my life.

I took more deep breaths.

And the feeling faded. The anxiety faded.

I was now able to control one out of every three, and it was the best fucking thing. Taking more deep breaths, I stood. I grabbed the wipes off the shelf and hurried back to Amanda. She saw me tucking the compass back into my pocket as I came into the living room. She was on the floor, changing the baby's diaper.

"You okay?" she asked, staring up at me.

"Great, actually. I almost had one, but it didn't happen."

"That's so amazing. Um, help."

"Shit." Literally. "I'll take the baby and clean her up. You clean that up." I made a face, dropping the wipes on the floor. Parenthood was about a million times harder than expected. But Amanda and I had been managing okay now that my mom had finally gone back to Maine. We made a good team. Actually, we made the best team.

I carefully grabbed the little one. She wasn't crying, so that was a plus for the moment. I'd be bawling my eyes out if I had shit my pants like she had. I took her out of the living room and straight to the kitchen sink. This was definitely a kitchen sink kind of moment. I got the water running and got her clean, right about the same moment Amanda finished cleaning up the mess in the living room. She washed her hands at the sink with me, muttering under her breath.

"Don't stress, baby," I whispered to her. I kissed her shoulder. "Lou should be here soon. We can have a small break then."

Lou and Finn arrived a few minutes later. Right on cue, they walked in without knocking. They were still dating and came over almost every evening. They often brought us dinner and helped to watch the baby. I hardly questioned their relationship anymore. Since having the baby, they'd quickly become our best friends. It wasn't like I was going to turn down dinner and help.

Even though I'd completely moved in here, Lou still hadn't left the rental. She'd taken over the payments. Every time I asked her about it, she told me not to worry about it. I think in reality, it was Finn making the payments. She seemed happy so I tried my best to stay out of her business.

"Thank you, God," I said when she walked in the door. The baby was clean and dry, in fresh new clothes, and I immediately plopped her into Lou's waiting arms. "Her bottle is in the fridge. I need a small break. Amanda needs a small break. Can you all manage for fifteen minutes?"

"Sure."

"We can manage for thirty," Finn added.

"Thank you."

I took Amanda's hand in mine and led her down the hallway. I didn't care what we did for the next thirty minutes. If we slept, if we showered, or if we fucked—I didn't care. I just needed her to myself for a while. Babies were a lot of work. A lot of *constant* work. And as much as I loved the time we spent as a family of three, taking these small moments alone was also something I needed, something we both needed.

I softly closed the door to our bedroom.

I turned into Amanda. Catching her face in my hands, I kissed her. I breathed her in. I loved her so much, sometimes it physically made me ache. My whole world was under this roof. I was so happy on that random Wednesday night I had decided I needed a turtle tattoo on my ass.

~ BONUS CHAPTER 1 ~

AMANDA

My heart would not stop hammering. I hated this. I hated that we'd been invited to this wedding, that we shared mutual friends with the bride and groom, that I had to be here tonight. Lou and Finn were babysitting Mia, which was incredibly sweet of them, and God knows I needed a night off, but right now I would have much rather been at home with our baby girl tucked in my arms. A shame too because Nick was in a tux.

A mother freaking tux.

This man with his rich, dark hair, and his amazing blue eyes, a jaw you could break ice on, should not be allowed in public in a tux. Or in the sun. The sun seemed to be amplifying his handsomeness. Caleb Mills, the man's whose wedding we were about to attend, was ridiculously famous. I should have realized sooner that attending a rockstar's wedding meant there might be other famous people in attendance. Other incredibly gorgeous, *model-level beautiful*, famous celebrity women who could not keep their eyes off of my guy.

We stood in line waiting to get into the church. Servers were handing out champagne to people heading inside. Nick pulled his gray beanie out from a pocket inside his tux jacket. I hadn't known he'd brought it with him. He tugged it on his head, covering his hair. It had been a long time since I'd seen him wear it. I loved him in that hat. But I also knew that he didn't wear it as a fashion statement or because it was cold. Today it was warm. He wore it more as a security of sorts.

On the outside he seemed calm. The hat told me on the inside he was anything but. I wanted to distract him. And my heart steadied because I knew I needed to.

"Nick."

"Yes?"

"There's something I've been wanting to show you. It's a new tattoo I recently got."

He had his hands in his pockets now. His eyes were on me. "Where at?" he said softly. His tone went low, just for me. "How did I miss it?"

"I've been careful not to let you see."

"Why?"

"It's a surprise. Um, well, it was supposed to be a surprise. But then I felt a little anxious about getting it."

"I need to see it. We should go."

"It's Emma's wedding."

"I'm only here for you." He took a breath. When we got the invitation, I hadn't asked him what he thought about being invited. He seemed unfazed, so I said we should go. I didn't want him to think it bothered me at all, being invited, attending the wedding of his ex. But it kind of did. I know he loved me fiercely, but that didn't mean I really wanted him to see Emma, who was stunning, in a white wedding dress today.

"I don't have to be here," I said.

"Yeah, me either."

"You never said you didn't want to come."

"I never said I did. Then you bought that dress."

"This one?"

He dipped close to my ear. "Yes. You are too beautiful in that dress. It would have been a fucking shame not to come, not to see you in it. It was worth it. It was worth the anxiety to see you in that dress."

I grabbed his hand in mine. "Come on."

He followed, no hesitation.

If he didn't want to be here, I didn't want to be here. We walked back toward the parking lot. As we moved through the crowded lot of cars, back toward where his car was parked on the end, he pulled me in close to his side. "I want to see your tattoo."

"I'm afraid you're going to hate it."

"Why?"

"If you hate it..." We reached his car. I stopped walking and turned to face him. "I will totally have Finn change it. He thinks he can. He thinks I should, actually. He told me it was cliché."

"Where is it?"

"Somewhere kind of private."

"Show me."

I rolled my eyes. "Fine." Nobody was in the parking lot. I could hear music from the church. Emma was probably walking down the aisle right this very moment.

My black dress was floor length with an exceptionally long slit running down my right leg. At the slit, I pulled it up, turning to show him my ass. I'd worn a thong, so my skin was already on display. I'd gotten the horrible turtle he'd originally picked out. The one I'd talked him out of. And I'd gotten it on my ass. I'd joked about it a while back, teasing him about finding his 'turtle-ass-soulmate.' I could have had Finn ink a turtle like Nick's design onto my skin. But for it to count, it needed to be the cliché one.

"It was a lame idea, right?"

I stared at him with my heart racing.

"Get in the car."

Great. He was annoyed. "I'm sorry. I can have Finn change it."

"No. I like it. Get in the car."

Okay, that was not an 'annoyed Nick voice.' That was his *'I'm going to try to get you pregnant all over again'* voice.

I got in the car.

~ BONUS CHAPTER 2 ~

NICK

Ugh. It was too hot. It was March and it was too hot, the sun beating on my back in my black tux. I hadn't worn this tux in a year or two and it was a little tight through the shoulders and arms now, adding to my discomfort. Amanda looked stunning though. He pink hair was pulled back, high on her head, with little pieces falling on her neck. I swear, I'd never found a neck so fucking sexy. I wanted to wrap my hands around her neck—kiss her, touch her, more than touch her. The ink on her shoulder, the colors and flowers, the tiny strawberries mixed it. Seventeen. That was how many small strawberries she had on her body. I'd secretly counted them. I'd found them all. They did things to me every time I saw them.

I pulled at my gray beanie. I tugged it on. I didn't feel uncomfortable having to go to Emma and Caleb's wedding, but I didn't exactly feel comfortable either.

"Nick."

"Yes?"

"There's something I've been wanting to show you. It's a new tattoo I recently got."

I pushed my hands into my pockets. I knew all her tattoos. I wouldn't have missed one. "Where at? How did I miss it?"

"I've been careful not to let you see."

"Why?"

"It's a surprise. Um, well, it was supposed to be a surprise. But then I felt a little anxious about getting it."

Her cheeks flushed. She's never been bashful about her ink before. God, the blush on her cheeks was going to make me hard moments before I had to walk into a church. "I need to see it. We should go."

"It's Emma's wedding."

"I'm only here for you."

"I don't have to be here."

"Yeah, me either." I so fucking didn't have to be here.

"You never said you didn't want to come."

"I never said I did. Then you bought that dress."

"This one?"

I moved closer to her, barely aware of the other people around us. "Yes. You are too beautiful in that dress. It would have been a fucking shame not to come, not to see you in it. It was worth it. It was worth the anxiety to see you in that dress."

She stared up a me for a moment, her big brown eyes on mine. Then she grabbed my hand and pulled me away from the line of people waiting to go into that crowded church. "Come on."

I followed. I was hers, I followed her so damn easily. We walked back through the parking lot. Her ass in that dress had my skin on fire. The moment we reached my car I pulled her close to my side. "I want to see your tattoo."

"I'm afraid you're going to hate it."

"Why?"

"If you hate it..." She turned to face me. "I will totally have Finn change it. He thinks he can. He thinks I should, actually. He told me it was cliché."

Finn. Fuck, Finn. Okay, we were friends now. But I didn't want him touching Amanda in any capacity. "Where is it?"

"Somewhere kind of private."

Motherfucker. Finn put it in a private place. "Show me."

"Fine." She tugged up the side of her black dress, displaying her leg, and then her round little ass cheek. My mouth was practically watering, seeing her skin in the sun.

On her cheek was a tennis-ball sized turtle tattoo. The very tattoo I'd picked for myself. The one she'd criticized. The one she'd joked about. Saying whatever girl I found it on would be my 'turtle-ass-soulmate.' I loved it. She'd marked herself as mine with this tattoo.

"It was a lame idea, right?"

"Get in the car," I muttered.

"I'm sorry. I can have Finn change it."

"No. I like it. Get in the car."

She heard the fire in my voice, the urgency. She opened the door and climbed in over the driver's seat. I followed, slamming my door shut behind us. I started the car and got the air conditioning going. I tugged off my beanie, tossing it aside. Then I moved to work off my tux jacket. Then I unbuttoned my shirt a little, slowly.

She watched.

I removed the cummerbund.

She watched.

I was hard and breathing heavy. I needed her here and now. "I love your new tattoo. I love you. Get over here."

She inched up her dress, moved across the console, and came to straddle my lap. I freed my cock, which ached like mad for my beautiful woman. She pulled her underwear to the side and inched down on me. I kissed her at the same moment.

She was wet and warm—pure heaven. My heaven. If I got arrested right now, I wouldn't even care. I loved her so much. She was the mother of my daughter, the woman who knew every side of me, who made me a better man, and one day I'd make her my wife.

I loved her tattoo.

She'd forever be my turtle-ass-soulmate.

THE END

* * *

ALSO BY SARAH DARLINGTON

The Never Trust Series

Never Trust a Rockstar

Never Kiss a Rockstar

Never Love a Rockstar

Never Leave a Rockstar

Kill Devil Hills Series

Kill Devil Hills

Changing Tides

Pulled Under

Adrift

Kill Devil Ink Series

Crazed

Inked

Marked

Standalones

He Belongs with Me

Leo Maddox

But First, Coffee

Owen

ABOUT THE AUTHOR

Sarah Darlington was born in Colorado and grew up all over the United States. These days, she calls Virginia home, where she lives with her husband, two kids, and large dog. The best word to describe Sarah is 'creative.' She's passionate about designing, crafting, and photography. But most of all... she loves creating stories through her writing.

Her romance books are sexy and heart-gripping at their core, guaranteed to make you swoon. Any of them can be read as a stand-alone, but all are connected within the same world.

sarahdarlingtonauthor.com

Made in the USA
Columbia, SC
09 January 2024

30176627R00137